Ian Rowlands was born in  and was educated at Ysgol trained as an actor at the Welsh College of Music and Drama, Cardiff. He is currently Artistic Director of Theatr y Byd and Artistic Coordinator of Theatr Bara Caws. As a writer his theatre credits include *The Sin-Eaters* (1992), *Solomon's Glory* (1993), *Glissando on an Empty Harp* (1994), *Love in Plastic* (1996), *Marriage of Convenience* (1997), which won an Angel Award at the Edinburgh Festival and The Dublin Dry Gin Award for Best Production at the Dublin Festival. *Blue Heron in the Womb* was produced in 1998, as a co-production between Theatr y Byd and The Tron Theatre, Glasgow and forms the final play in The Trilogy of Appropriation.

He has also written extensively for radio and television; his work includes *A Light in the Valley*, which won the Royal Television Society Award for Best Regional Drama in 1999. Other work includes *The Ogpu Men, TV a'r Wal* and for radio *3 o'clock at Ponty* and *Dough Boys*, as well as a substantial number of programmes for BBC Radio Education.

He lives in Cardiff.

PARTHIAN BOOKS

A Trilogy of Appropriation

Three plays

Ian Rowlands

PARTHIAN BOOKS

Parthian Books
53 Colum Road
Cardiff
CF1 3EF

First published in 1999.

All rights reserved.

Copyright Ian Rowlands

ISBN 1-902638-01-8

The publishers would like to thank the Arts Council of Wales for support in the publication of this book.

Printed and bound by ColourBooks, Dublin 13, Ireland.

With support from the Parthian Collective.

Typeset in Galliard by NW.

Cover Design by Savage.

A CIP catalogue record for this book is available from the British Library.

This book is sold subject to the condition that it shall not by way of trade or otherwise be circulated without the publisher's prior consent in any form of binding or cover other than that in which it is published and without a similar condition including the condition being imposed on the subsequent purchaser.

I SHARON

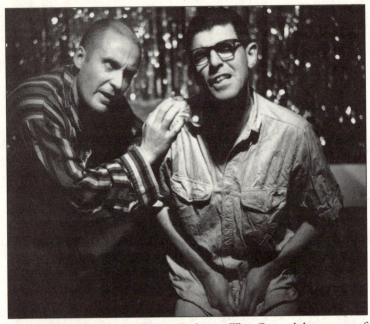

Ian Rowlands & Dafydd Wyn Roberts, The Great Adventures of Rhys and Hywel (photo Dave Heke)

CONTENTS

A Decade of Debt Ian Rowlands 9

A BLUE HERON IN THE WOMB 15

Thoughts on a play Irina Brown 85

LOVE IN PLASTIC 87

Thoughts on a play Jill Piercy 160

GLISSANDO ON AN EMPTY HARP 165

Thoughts on a play Declan Gorman 235

Theatr y Byd Production History 238

Retrospective David Adams 241

All is Sign
  after Eco

A DECADE OF DEBT

I could wax lyrical, a Welsh dramatist's greatest atribute according to some, about the linguistic play within my work (I come from the Rhondda Valley - where the Welsh language is still spoken but through the medium of English), I could trace the influence of Commedia dell Arte upon my vision of theatre and qualify my experiments in cross media pollination, but that's a history best chronicled by others. What I can do is to outline Theatr y Byd's history which has in essence been a history of thank-yous.

In the beginning was the car and the car was Dafydd Wyn Roberts and Dafydd Wyn Roberts was the car. Without the car nothing would've been possible. One damp afternoon a decade ago, driving towards Tregaron, a West Walian frontier town, Dafydd was theorising about the throwback nature of the Tregaron residents, how, having been cut off from civilisation for centuries by a marsh, they were in essence Neanderthal. (Later I was to find an essay in the National Library that set out to disprove this). I kept an open mind. We stopped at the petrol station in the centre of the village. I filled up the car and went into the kiosk to pay. Two minutes later I came running out shouting 'My God, you're right. His forehead was that big!'. And on that garage forecourt in Tregaron, Theatr y Byd was conceived.

Some months later in the back bar of the Old New Inn, Llanfyllin, Rhys Rhys, the balding git and Hywel ap Dafydd, life's great disappointment, the alter egos of Dafydd and myself, stepped onto the stage. Thanks to Cordie and Jenny for dragging their friends along to that first night and for their support in the years that followed.

The one act play we performed that first night, *In Search of Tregaron Man* was a surreal sideswipe at contemporary life in Wales. Within a year or so, parts two to four of the now titled *The Great Adventures of Rhys and Hywel, In Search of Tregaron Man,*

Jean and MI9, *Something Comes of Nothing* and *Consumatum Est*, were performed on four consecutive Sundays at the Four Bars Inn in Cardiff (now called Dempsy's, poised to be Cardiff's first pub theatre as I write). A big thanks to all who joined the adventure, but mostly to Rob Lane for his rash commitment. Paying for the tickets out of our own pockets, we also took the ferry to Ireland and performed parts two and three at The Triskel Arts Centre, Cork. Ger O'Riordan, the then theatre programmer of the Triskel, was our first friend in Ireland, a country whose support has been instrumental in the company's development.

Theatr y Byd's first funded production was a co-production with Wales Actors' Company. Directed by Ruth Garnault, both Paul Garnault and Rachel Atkins joined Rhys and Hywel for *The Sin Eaters*, a full length, fifth part of the *Great Adventures* which toured Wales, Ireland and Brittany in 1992. ('Nominated Best Regional theatre Play for 1992' by The Writers' Guild of GB). Stephen Young, the Cardiff based artist, created a suite of drawing of the company in rehearsal and an exhibition of this work toured with the production.

The company's first major tour in its own right was *Solomon's Glory* which premiered at The City Arts Centre, Dublin, in January 1993. It toured Wales, England, Scotland, France and Ireland; ten weeks of madness on a budget of less than eleven thousand pounds. Many thanks are due to the following for their support both on *Solomon's Glory* and subsequent tours; in Ireland, Declan Gorman and all at the City Arts (including Liam), Marie and Maura - Linenhall Arts Centre Castlebar, Jo Murphy - St John's Arts Centre Listowel, Michael Diskin - Town Hall Theatre, Galway, John and Phil Cleere - Cleere's Theatre Kilkenny. In Brittany, Marianne Correge, Bernard Siche and Jean Christophe at Carrefour de l'Europe. In Wales John Lightwood & all at Llanover Hall, Mr and Mrs Bickford - Llandegla, Mrs. Lambert -Y Tabernacl Machynlleth, Jackie Pallit for the great curry- Queen's Hall, Narberth, Marie Majors - Berwyn Centre, Nantymoel, The Crystals - Ucheldre Centre, Holyhead and Phil Clark - Artistic Director of

The Sherman Theatre and current chair of Theatr y Byd's board.

To Winston Evans, Iwan John, Gareth Potter and Chris Morgan, the actors who gave their all for ten pounds a show, and to Stephen Young, Andy Dark, Dave Heke, Linda Brown and Emma Lawton whose art inspired solely by the text inspired the production - Diolch o galon.

Why open what was intrinsically a profit share production in Dublin on the 26th January 1993? Because by the morning of the 27th we had five national reviews. We would have been lucky to have got the *Western Mail* in Wales and unfortunately, it is still the case!

In 1994 we toured *Glissando on an Empty Harp* around the increasingly familiar Celtic circuit. (A big thanks in part to the Manx man at the British Council in Dublin, Harold Fish, whose continued commitment to an obscure Welsh company has been much appreciated) The Irish artist Martina Galvin created an installation within which an integral part of the production was filmed by Terry Dimmick and Dave Heke. *Glissando* is one of the high points for the company, for though it played to more people in two nights in Nantes than it did in the whole of the Welsh leg of its tour, it was one hell of a 'craic'. If Theatr y Byd's history is a history of thank-yous, it's because so much was achieved on so little. Another four-country tour was mounted on a budget of seventeen thousand, a quarter of which was used to realise the multi-media element. The commitment of the actors and crew was vital both to the production and the further legitimisation of Theatr y Byd on the Welsh theatrical scene.

After *Glissando*, the company mounted *Quartet* - four monologues which toured in Rep around Wales during the Autumn of 1994. *Thinking in Welsh* performed and written by Dafydd Wyn Roberts, *The Change* by Jane Buckler and Helen Griffin, performed by Helen Griffin, *Big Black Hole* by Tim Rhys performed by Richard Nichols and the much acclaimed *Gobeithion Gorffwyll* by Simone de Beauvoir translated and performed by Sharon Morgan (premiered at Y Tabernacl, Machynlleth). An exhibition entitled *Portrait and Portrayal* was mounted in the Owen Owen Gallery in Y Tabernacl to coincide with the production. The idea behind this third experiment in 'cross media pollination' was to pair four artists off with four actors to create portraits of 'portrayers'. Tony Goble was paired with Dafydd Wyn Roberts, Sue Williams with Helen Griffin, Gareth Davies with Richard Nichols and Catrin Jones (the recipient of the Theatr y Byd award at the Eisteddfod Genedlaethol that year) with Sharon Morgan.

Love in Plastic written with only the second bursary of its kind awarded by the Arts Council of Wales, premiered at the Glynn Vivian Gallery, Swansea. The project was unique as it combined several elements; the text was published with the assistance of the Swansea Year of Literature, a retrospective of Theatr y Byd's 'Experiments in multi media' was mounted at the Glynn Vivian Gallery which comprised all art work commissioned by the company to date plus an installation inspired by the text created by conceptual artist, Tim Davies. Allison Lloyd, the gallery programmer, deserves a big thanks for inviting us to present such a unique project in the gallery. To facilitate Tim's work with the company, Theatr y Byd was the first theatre company in Wales to be given money to employ an artist in residence. This was facillitated by Carwyn Rogers at West Wales Arts. Both Carwyn and his late dear wife Beth had been friends of Theatr y Byd from the beginning; diolch i chi'ch ddau.

Following a four-week exhibition, the fourth wall of Tim Davies' installation was taken out and *Love in Plastic* was performed within the work of art; the artist had reacted with the text in order to create an installation, in performance the actors interacted with the art. A touring production of this followed in May 1996.

Marriage of Convenience, the company's next major production, was a case of necessity's child. Originally conceived as a four-hander, *Marriage of Convenience* was commissioned and funded under the first 'Season of Work' initiative by the Arts

Council of Wales. The other production to be staged by Theatr y Byd in the season was the first ever translation of a two-hander by Michelle Tremblay. However, after consideration, it was decided that it would be more beneficial to translate a four-hander *Cendres de Cailloux*, the work of another Quebecois dramatist, Daniel Danis. Gareth Miles' crafted adaptation, *Lludw'r Garreg*, toured to much critical acclaim in the Spring of 1997.

The consequence of choosing to mount *Lludw'r Garreg* with its larger than budgeted for cast, meant that *Marriage of Convenience* had to be a smaller cast piece and a four-hander was reduced to a monologue almost overnight.

It opened on a stormy day in Coleg Meirion Dwyfor, Dolgellau. Gareth Potter, the fool who'd challenged the mountain of words and conquered it, had travelled along with the crew to Dolgellau the previous day. Both Dafydd Wyn Roberts and myself stayed in Llanfyllin the night before as we had to deliver publicity posters en route. When we woke up the next morning the world was blanketed in snow. All in all, it took ten hours to travel between Llanfyllin and Dolgellau. We had to make a détour of a hundred miles via England, across North Wales and back down the west coat to reach Dolgellau, a mere forty miles from Llanfyllin as the crow flies. We arrived at the theatre with a quarter an hour to spare before curtain up. An auspicious opening to what has since proved to be the company's most successful production to date. It has completed three major tours, won an 'Angel' award at the Edinburgh Festival, Gareth was also nominated 'Best Actor' in the Stage awards at Edinburgh that year. It then went on to win the 'Dublin Dry Gin award for Best Production at the Dublin Festival' and was performed at the British Festival of Visual Theatre in 1997.

With *Marriage of Convenience* we first developed our association with The Tron Theatre, Glasgow. We think it was hiraeth that possessed the general manager of The Tron, Neil Murray, a good Newport boy, to blindly book us in. However, following our run at the theatre, Irina Brown, the Tron's Artistic Director, invited the company to collaborate with The Tron upon

Blue Heron in the Womb which premiered in Glasgow in May 1998. A tour of Wales followed in the Spring of 1999.

There are many more people to thank, but this is a volume of plays not one of handshakes and air kisses. To all those who have not been named, thank you for support down the years, you have helped turn a thinly veiled excuse for international drinking into a serious player on the Welsh theatrical scene. In particular, I would like to personally thank Dave Roxburgh (Production co-ordinator), Liz Cowling (Secretary to the board) and Sarah Argent (Marketing) whose combined skills have professionalised the company, and Lawson Dando whose haunting music has added so much to the company's productions.

Lastly, this *Trilogy of Appropriation* would never have been written were it not for the inspiration of one woman, Sharon Morgan. Her influence has shaped my life more than any other... diolch o galon.

IAN ROWLANDS i.99

Blue Heron in the Womb

Blue Heron in the Womb was first performed at the Tron Theatre, Glasgow on the 21st of May 1998.

Cast

MAN - **Jonathan Nefydd**
SISTER - **Liz Armon-Lloyd**
WOMAN - **Catrin Powell**
MOTHER - **Siân Rivers**
FATHER - **Eilian Wyn**

director **Ian Rowlands**
designer - **Sean Crowley**
stage manager - **Darryl James**
lighting design / - **David Roxburgh**
production manager
marketing / publicity - **Sarah Argent**
adinistration - **Liz Cowling**

This version of the play toured Wales in 1999. Betsan Llwyd played mother.

A MAN HOVERS SIX FEET ABOVE WALES

MAN	The first thing she said when her new born child screamed upon her breast was 'Fuck it! So much pain and he's going to die like the rest of us.' Of course, she didn't know how soon his death would come, no one did. Her wildest stab would have been way off the mark, her child died much sooner than the pessimist predicted.
Mind you, it could have been worse, he could've grown old enough to have stopped off for a piss in Pasadena, had his cock cut off by a Hell's Angel's blade and bled to death upon the pissy tiles... He didn't.
There again, as a grown man, his soul could've cankered quicker than his yellowing flesh as he watched his own son play, knowing that he would never talk the talk over a pint. Or past reason and desperate, he could've greeted the Avon mud from the height of Clifton Bridge, but that would've necessitated the child growing tall enough to straddle the railings.
By the time he died, he'd barely straddled into being; there was still a dispute over his name. His coffin was minute.
Consumed by flames, it yielded barely a handful of ash to convince the world that a child had once struggled to focus upon a pessimist's face. But it had, with Burundi eyes, the nameless one had named himself as hungry bugger junior; the last in a long line of hungry buggers on his father's side; but his mother never talked about them in the fist fuck of her family, that would have been indecent in polite company.

A FAMILY DRESSED IN UNDERWEAR PREPARE FOR A JOURNEY. THE WOMEN OF THE FAMILY SERVICE THE FATHER'S NEEDS BEFORE THEIR OWN. THE SISTER AND WOMAN IRON HIS CLOTHES. THE MOTHER PREPARES A PICNIC.

SISTER His jeans were so tight I thought he'd painted them on. I could see his cock; vacuum packed, balls visible both sides of the seam. He had a pony tail and a leather jacket ...

WOMAN You got in a car with a pony tail!

SISTER I needed to get there

WOMAN How old was he?

SISTER Does it matter?

WOMAN Was he past forty?

SISTER I didn't ask. I kept my lips and my legs tightly crossed all the way from Caernarfon to Cardiff. Even when I screamed, I screamed silence

WOMAN Why, what happened?

SISTER Pulling out of the Little Chef in Dolgellau, as he changed from first to second, he brought his hand to rest on the hand brake, up until then, it had rested solely upon his knee; second to third, he placed it on the edge of my seat; third to fourth, he rested it palm down close to my leg. Even then, I said nothing... I just melted. Moulding myself around the door handle; calculating the potential damage to a body hitting the tarmac at seventy miles an hour; the flesh that would tear, the bones that would break

WOMAN   You should've said something?

SISTER   It was too late to walk

WOMAN   You should've caught the bus

SISTER   I couldn't afford the ticket

WOMAN   I would rather have crawled on glass

SISTER   Well, you are you, and I am me. We are twins, Lizzy; The same but different

WOMAN   Exactly

SISTER   But not quite

WOMAN   Do you always have to have the last word, Chrissy?

SISTER   I was last out

FATHER   Girls..

BOTH   Sorry, Dada

MOTHER CUTS THE CRUSTS OFF WHITE BREAD

MOTHER   I've learnt negativity from you, my husband, as most women do. I adopted your values and adapted my life for the sake of peace. And so, on the outside, your values became 'our' values, but inside, I've lived by a hidden code... in camera emotions, all these years. I suppose you could call that hypocrisy, but that would be the vocabulary of a different generation. Of course I've never doubted your intention, not to your face, I've never wanted to hurt you, so I kept mum when your obsession with 'your' girls, particularly Lizzy, stifled... negated...ignored. Not that I suspected anything untoward, mind you... but, it was a passion that eclipsed the love we had once shared. That hurt, Huw, that hurt.

So guilty, so over the moon when we found out Lizzy was pregnant... you weren't. I've never clung to the purity of a white wedding as you have, I wish I'd played the field a bit before settling down, known other men... been able to draw comparison... but in our day it wasn't the fashion, was it, Huw?

FATHER Slaving away, mother?

MOTHER With a smile upon my face, Huw, always with a smile

WE HEAR THE TWINS' THOUGHTS AS THEY DRESS THEIR FATHER

SISTER It's weird how the world periscopes when your crotch moistens and your pupils dilate; how the peripheries soft focus into the object. Like walking down the tunnel in Green Park with *Laudate Dominus* on the Walkman; the sensual intensity, the focus finite.
It was over lunch I first noticed you, playing chess with your vegetarian option. I caught your eye as it flew past me forcing the smile, 'Coffee?' you mouthed. 'Coffee would be 'nice'.'
Alex, a name never whispered in our house, why the hell did I fall for you; a third year art student who'd once stood in the rain for twenty four hours to see if

your face would melt? It didn't, any fool could've told you that; only you would've felt the need to have proved it

WOMAN   You stood on my doorstep in Aberystwyth; Chrissy dangling from limp fingers, a bottle of Chardonnay held in a tight fist. 'This is he,' she said. That night in The Crystal Palace, you held the undivided attention of twins. You said it was 'like masturbating in a mirrored lift.'

SISTER A mad, bad godhead of a boy, your energy was infectious, your bum delicious. That night, we made a week of it, drinking our way around the Pontcanna Triangle; Conway, Half Way and Cameo until morning was born out of night.
And not wanting to part, we headed off to the park for a swing and roundabout night cap, and in the dark, my tongue probed your artistic nature, and you loved it...

WOMAN   Later, walking home along the prom, the sea air blew your legs apart, you lay lengthwise in a gutter being sick into a grating. She just picked you up and kissed you as if you'd been lying in snow sucking mints. I could never have done that. I guess that was the big difference between us, she could lick sick, I couldn't.

SISTER You can love your twin, it doesn't mean you have to like her; little Miss Prissy Bitch, the golden delicious in dada's eye; I was always the sty, the irritant. She was always the favourite, the one the greatest hopes were reserved for; I lived on scraps of comfort thrown my way out of pity, nothing great was expected from me, but she, was the Deb of a nation; her Welsh was immaculate, her womb - consecrated. Dada expected the utmost from her...

SHE TURNS TO WOMAN

SISTER   ... It's why her downfall was so perfect

SISTER STARES AT WOMAN

WOMAN   Chrissy?

SISTER   Nothing

WOMAN   Cardiff at short notice and Chrissy wasn't around. 'If you had nowhere to stay, you should've said'. But it had only been three months since you'd split up with my sister and I felt the scar might still be delicate. 'I am healed', you pronounced, but it was obvious that the wound hadn't quite closed; mind you, most wounds tend to re-open after a few pints.
After the fourth, you declared 'If you have nowhere to stay, stay with me tonight'. It's odd how the world turns on half words in the moonlight.
You offered your bed 'No' I protested', 'Please' you implored until I felt you actually meant it. 'Tell you what, why don't we share the bed, and I promise no funny stuff' I didn't trust you, you'd made love to Chrissy, but that was part of the attraction, I guess. That night, we huddled like animals closing for warmth. I felt so cosy, wrapped in arms that already knew me, I stayed an extra night. Six weeks later I was pregnant.

ONLY THE FATHER IS DRESSED

FATHER   Ready?

MOTHER   Patience is the mother of all wisdom, Huw

FATHER   What have you been doing?

WOMAN   Wasting my time

FATHER   You'd better get a move on

THE WOMEN DRESS

SISTER   I found out you were an 'item' through a mutual friend, it's odd how friends relish disaster with an understanding tongue. 'Hasn't your sister mentioned it?' She knew damn well she hadn't. 'How embarrassing' she blushed delight.
'I don't give a fuck' I said, but inside, I screamed. I didn't know whether to blame Lizzy or you, the little shit who'd reached out for the penny and the bun, the bastard who shagged the cake then ate it.

WOMAN   'I want to be immortal' you proclaimed one afternoon walking up Constitution Hill towards the Camera Obscura. 'Help me live forever... will you... please Lizzy? I glanced up at your hair, already thinning at twenty-three. 'You can't live for ever' I said, searching Ireland on the horizon. 'I can Lizzy, if you love me. Love cheats death, any pint pot poet can tell you that.' Perhaps you're right... had you been there at your grandfather's death you could've faced the fear, but your mother pulled you away too soon. Because I loved you, I wanted to help you tame your fear by giving it a home in my womb; a home where your dreams of eternity could take substance and grow. Sitting my finals four months gone, how I got a two one I'll never know?

FATHER   You would've got a first if it wasn't for him

WOMAN   Pardon, Dada?

FATHER   Just thinking out loud. You were first material, Lizzy, heading for an MA and a doctorate

MOTHER   A two one is excellent, Huw

FATHER   As Nain used to say, 'Not good where dwells the better'

MOTHER   A miracle, considering

FATHER   A disaster

SISTER   It could've been worse, Dada, it could've been a two two

FATHER   God forbid

MOTHER   A passable degree

FATHER   Not worth the paper it's printed on

SISTER   But worth the memory

FATHER   I don't want to know how you earned your badge of shame, Chrissy. You may wear failure with pride but it ill suits Lizzy.

MOTHER   Huw!

FATHER   Nothing hurts like the truth, mother.

MOTHER   But sometimes it's better not to state it

FATHER   To state is my prerogative

MOTHER   Please, Huw, today is difficult enough as it is

FATHER   Isn't it just; a trial to be endured! Remember, my girl, truth is a patient sentinel.

SISTER   (UNDER HER BREATH) I can hardly wait

FATHER   Is everything ready, mother?

MOTHER   Yes

FATHER   The kitchen sink?

MOTHER   Packed

FATHER   That just leaves the little one, I'll take care of him

HE PICKS UP THE URN CONTAINING THE CHILD'S ASHES

FATHER   Best foot forward then

THEY JOURNEY TO THE MOUNTAIN TOP

MAN   The oak had been standing for two hundred years, two centuries of summer rings, two hundred winters waiting. Alex glanced at his favourite tree, rooted in the centre of the mushroom field, as he drove past it on his way to the city to do some unnecessaries that could've waited.
When he left around ten, there was barely a breeze to flutter the dragon in a Nationalist's garden, by midday, the storm had kicked in. Around four, business

done, phone lines down, he hammered West along the M4. A few miles from home, he turned into the valley and drove past the splintered victims of the storm, hacked and cleared from the road just in time; he had to wait for the last casualty to be operated upon. In the tempest, his favourite tree had been torn up and flung down

THE FATHER NEARLY DROPS THE URN

FATHER   Dear God, I nearly dropped him

THE FAMILY STEADY HIM

MAN   When he arrived, he found a woman in labour, crying by a dead phone 'Where the hell have you been?' she screamed, 'they're coming thick and fast.' 'My God. Keep breathing'. Minutes later, they were driving past the limbless dead, half an hour later they were in the maternity ward, three hours later their child was born with a snip of skin, six hours later, driving home on his own, he kept thinking 'What the fuck is it all about?'. He stopped his car beside the mushroom field, and in the morgue of the night, he climbed onto the corpse of his favourite tree, and cried

ARRIVING ON THE MOUNTAIN TOP. THE FATHER SURVEYS WALES THROUGH BINOCULARS

FATHER   I'd rather be dead than be Dutch. If you can't put your country into perspective from the top of a mountain, how can you love it, I say?

MOTHER   The Dutch are an enterprising nation, Huw

FATHER   Perhaps they are, but their landscape is vertically thwarted. You can not, whatever anyone says, you can not belong to a land as flat as pancakes. Mountains are the memory of a nation written in stone, without them there is neither longing nor belonging. I pity the Dutch and I pray for them.

MOTHER   (TO HERSELF) A nation will sleep easy tonight. (TO WOMAN) Sandwich?

WOMAN   Not for me

MOTHER   But you're eating for two

WOMAN   Not at the moment

MOTHER   Chrissy?

SISTER   On a diet

MOTHER   Father?

FATHER   Later perhaps? Do you remember, the last time we stood here? It when when we scattered Nain's ashes. Do you remember, mother?

MOTHER   With affection, Huw

FATHER   Shame you never got on

MOTHER EATS ONE SANDWICH THEN RE-PACKS THE REST

WOMAN   After my degree, I exiled myself in your dream; an isolated cottage three miles from the nearest town. The day of the storm...

THE NEXT TWO SPEECHES ARE SPOKEN
SIMULTANEOUSLY.

WOMAN   I sat alone watching the crows tacking upon a Cape wind, listening to the whip crack of trees splitting. On the television, the weather forecast worsened from minute to minute. I wondered whether you'd be able to get home that night and whether your business couldn't have waited? Inside me, our baby was dying to get out...Around three I felt my first contraction... At half three the phone was cut off...Around four, panic began to set in. You arrived around five thirty, immediately we left for the hospital. I knelt doggie in the back of the car, hoping between contractions that all your talk of abortion and adoption would end that night. I kept thinking of a conversation eighteen years on - 'Was I an accident?' 'Not at all' I'd answer, hand on heart, no accident...

SISTER   We lunched together; Greek salad and cappuccino in one of the new café bars that kid Cardiff it's a Capital city. We'd arranged to meet because things had been left unsaid and that afternoon would be our last opportunity to intimately say sour nothings to each other; the sort of conversation school kids have with their best friend's boyfriend; dry words, wet lips. 'She really does love you' you re-assure him over and over again, closing in, ready to salve his pain with your tongue.
Harmonising with your cock and the clock, I screamed bitch songs at the top of my voice as revenge burst my clitoris. 'I love you' you said 'I wish it was you in Carmarthen not Lizzy'. 'Say nothing, just fuck me' I arched and sucked you in, drowning several dreams with one scream.

Sliding off my belly, you checked your watch. 'Shit' you sighed reaching for the phone; dialling once, dialling twice, dialling the operator; the phone line was down. 'This can never happen again' you pleaded, playing twister with your trousers 'Never again'. We both agreed, knowing in the twitch of a crotch that we would break our promises and repeat our oaths ad infinitum...

WOMAN ... but how could I tell our child that once conceived his father wished him forgotten or dead?

WOMAN LOOKS AS IF SHE IS ABOUT TO CRY

SISTER Lizzy?

WOMAN Too many thoughts for one small day... At sixteen weeks, a little life was a needle's breadth away from the bin. I lay on an operating table, you sat at my side, your Peter Pan wings pawned, re-assuring me that we had made the right decision. It was only when the hypodermic was that close that I said 'This is a mistake' 'Are you sure?' you asked pinning me down with your voice 'As sure as eggs crack'. 'It's your decision' you said for the nurse's benefit, but your eyes screamed 'Fuck it!' From then on, you talked adoption; a round tune on a cracked horn. Oh!

WOMAN PUTS HER HANDS TO HER STOMACH

SISTER All right?

WOMAN I felt a kick

SISTER Can I?

WOMAN   There

SISTER PUTS A HAND TO WOMAN'S STOMACH

SISTER   The Nine o'clock News showed a country blown apart; sandbags, smashed caravans and insurers calculating. Tucked away after the storms, another plane crash, another paedophile ring, life goes on

SISTER PUTS HER CHEEK TO THE WOMAN'S STOMACH

SISTER   I could still sense you hard inside me...I felt your sperm trickle out... I thought about having a bath, but didn't run it. Instead I tested the waters with my finger and tasted them. With your life in my mouth, I was certain that Lizzy had given birth, the same sort of feeling I had in my arm when Lizzy had broken hers; a knowing sort of feeling... a twin thing

WOMAN CARESSES BOTH HER TWIN AND HER STOMACH

WOMAN   When our little baby was taken to be weighed you let go of my hand; your knuckles, white with squeezing, and as you stood in awe of your little son tipping the scales, all your horror condensed in a tear upon your cheek... In a sterile delivery room, in the company of strangers, we were a family. Six weeks later, our baby was dead

SISTER LEAVES WOMAN. WOMAN ALMOST CRIES. MOTHER APPROACHES HER

MOTHER Penny for your thoughts

WOMAN   Have them for free

MOTHER Are you hurting?

WOMAN   I'm too angry

MOTHER Try not to upset yourself

WOMAN   I just want to get this over and done with, Mama?

MOTHER Tradition takes time, Lizzy

WOMAN   My baby sat dead on a mantelpiece longer than he lived.

MOTHER Ashes have always been kept for a year in your father's family, that's the way it is

WOMAN   Why?

MOTHER Out of respect

WOMAN   For the living or the dead?

MOTHER Break a tradition and you break an ancestor's heart

WOMAN   My heart is glass, dead hearts are stone!

MAN   It's probably only in the face of death, we truly live. Only then do we appreciate our lives, lifetimes too late. Of course a six-week-old baby is barely aware of life to miss it.
Had a baby lived he would've sledged down a garage drive at twelve, missed the sharp metal frame by a fraction, come to a stand still, and sat rigid with fear

having faced his mortality for the first time in his life.
Unfortunately our six-week-old baby was never given
the opportunity to learn that lesson.
He had not begun the process of naming the world
through identifying his fears. Therefore, he had no
name for the sharp needle of near translucence that
pierced his fontanelle killing him outright, he
probably didn't even have a final thought. The
thoughts were left to be thought by the living in their
hospital beds, the blame was silently attributed

THE FATHER OPENS THE URN, TAKES OUT A PINCH
OF ASH AND DURING THE PRAYER, SCATTERS HIS
DEAD GRANDCHILD TO THE FOUR WINDS

FATHER   Let us pray... They say babies gurgle in dialect,
rehearsing the language they will eventually speak. If
this is true, then Welsh babies are doubly blessed, for
their gurglings are not only the formative sounds of
the divine tongue, but their linguistic passports to life
everlasting

Of course, some lives are cut too too short; the loss of
a voice barely gurgled. But though we, the listening,
will carry the loss in our ears and in our hearts, let us
comfort ourselves with the knowledge that our dear
dear departed, prematurely lost to both us and our
nation, will gurgle with our Lord, and call him Dada in
the dragon's tongue, for Welsh truly is the language of
Heaven

MOTHER Amen

FATHER & CHRISSY

WOMAN   Oh God...

MOTHER   You should've been a preacher, father

FATHER   I look pasty in black

WOMAN IS CLOSE TO THE EDGE. SISTER APPROACHES

SISTER   It's a long way down

WOMAN   In Cardiff, just before Alex went to the Czech Republic, we were standing on the top balcony of the Capitol Centre looking at the pianist playing Waltzes two floors below. Alex was holding his little genius, tilting him over the abyss so that he could get a better view of the piano. I had this vision of Alex dropping our baby to his death, so I snatched my baby from him. I knew it was irrational, but it was a gut feeling; a moment of doubt, you know - a killing moment. That's when I knew that I didn't trust him, and that was the beginning of the end, I guess... Why did you leave him?

SISTER   Alex?

WOMAN   Yes

SISTER   Why?

WOMAN   Just curious

SISTER   To be honest, I forget

WOMAN   I don't believe that

SISTER   Believe what you want

WOMAN   The truth, Chrissy

SISTER The truth sticks in my gullet.

WOMAN   Please

SISTER On a day like this!

WOMAN   I need to hear it

SISTER Do you?

WOMAN   A lot of things don't make sense

SISTER Most things don't

WOMAN   Humour me

SISTER Not today

WOMAN   Today's as good a day as any. Why did you and Alex split?

PAUSE

SISTER He split, I exploded. The truth is... he left me

WOMAN   Why?

SISTER Oh... I don't know... Lots of shit

WOMAN   What shit?

SISTER Shit is shit

WOMAN   Be specific

SISTER I don't want to be

WOMAN   Chrissy

SISTER I don't want to hurt myself; I don't want to hurt you

WOMAN   I'm numb, I wouldn't feel a thing. I need the truth to feel again. Tell me... as twin to twin

SISTER Is the truth that important?

WOMAN   It is to me

BEAT

SISTER It was a case of taste actually. I stomached most of his crap, but then I stopped short...

WOMAN   ... short of what?

SISTER His cock and bullshit

WOMAN   Which bit?

SISTER His eternity trip. I couldn't swallow it

WOMAN   You talked eternity!

SISTER Surprised?

WOMAN   A bit

SISTER Sorry...

WOMAN   For you or for me?

SISTER   For us both

WOMAN   And I thought I was the special one

SISTER   Don't we all, Lizzy. Don't we all wish to taste 'forever' on our lips?

BEAT

WOMAN   Shit, Chrissy, why didn't you tell me this before?

SISTER   You never asked

WOMAN   Why tell me now?

SISTER   You demanded the truth

WOMAN   You could've lied

SISTER   And said what... that I was frigid, so he left me for the perfection he found between your legs

WOMAN   Please...

SISTER   He left me because I refused to give up my womb for the sake of his eternity, you, acquiesced. That's your precious truth, Lizzy

WOMAN   God, you're like Dada

SISTER   Don't

PAUSE

WOMAN   Do you hate him?

SISTER Dada?

WOMAN   Alex?

SISTER No

WOMAN   Do you still love him?

SISTER You've no right to ask that

WOMAN   Do you?

BEAT

WOMAN   Does he still love you?

SISTER Who cares?

WOMAN   I do. I'm the one carrying his second child. Does he still love you?

SISTER Probably not

WOMAN   But possibly?

SISTER Leave it, Lizzy?

WOMAN   Why?

SISTER What's past is past.

WOMAN   But it's not past, is it?

SISTER   Oh for God's sake...

WOMAN   Why are you getting so uptight?

SISTER   Why do you think?

WOMAN   Do you love him?

SISTER   You're being unfair

WOMAN   It's my day to be as unfair as I like. Do you still love him?

SILENCE

WOMAN   You do, don't you. And he probably does you, doesn't he. And you're still lovers, aren't you?

SISTER   Lizzy...

WOMAN   Does he pump you till the steam comes out of your ears? Does he, Chrissy?

SISTER   Don't...

WOMAN   Does he?

SISTER   For God's sake!

WOMAN   Do you still fuck? Do you still fuck, Chrissy?

SISTER   Did you? Or did you love as you sucked him deeper within ? Tell me...Did you fuck Chrissy? Tell me. Because if you did, then yes, we still fuck

WOMAN   Good. Now I can truly hate him

BEAT

SISTER   I love you, Lizzy

WOMAN   Love you too... but where do you end and I begin?

THEY HUG. WOMAN PULLS AWAY LEAVING SISTER AT THE CLIFF'S EDGE

FATHER   The reverend has bought two cottages and knocked them into one. Not that I doubt his devotion, mother, but though his pay is pious, his lifestyle is bordering on the Catholic...

WOMAN   Can we leave, please?

MOTHER   Sandwich, Lizzy?

WOMAN   No thanks

MOTHER   You must eat

WOMAN   I'm OK

FATHER   You know what happened last time, when you weren't taken care of properly

WOMAN   I'm not hungry

MOTHER   Try and nibble something

WOMAN   Why are you always trying to feed me Mama?

MOTHER We love you

WOMAN   Love lies in the heart, not the stomach

MOTHER Not always...especially past forty. Chrissy?

SISTER   What?

FATHER   Pardon, Chrissy

SISTER   Pardon, Mama?

MOTHER Would you like a little sandwich?

SISTER   I've lost my appetite

MOTHER Are you sure?

SISTER   Positive

MOTHER But it's egg... your favourite

SISTER   Was my favourite

MOTHER Was?

SISTER   Was

MOTHER Was is such a shame... Banana?

SISTER   No thanks

MOTHER Sure, Lizzy?

FATHER   Don't force her mother. You know what she's like, as soon as you start eating she'll want some

SISTER   No I won't, Dada

FATHER   We'll see

SISTER   I won't

MOTHER   You might feel peckish later...

WOMAN   The train leaves in five minutes, Mama, I think we should catch it

MOTHER   So soon?

FATHER   Time stalks the righteous

SISTER   I want to stay a bit longer

MOTHER   I wish we could...

FATHER   ...but we can't.

MOTHER   Perhaps we could come here some day without the dead. Father?

FATHER   We'll talk about it

MOTHER GOES TO SISTER

MOTHER   You all right, Chrissy?

SISTER   Leave me here, Mama

MOTHER   I can't do that

SISTER   I need to be alone

MOTHER   At this moment?

SISTER   This moment

FATHER   What's wrong, Mother?

MOTHER   Nothing, Huw...

SISTER   ...I'm not catching the train, Dada

FATHER   There's no time to walk

SISTER   I'm not walking, I'm staying

FATHER   Chrissy. We came as a family, we shall leave as a family

SISTER   We came alone, and we shall leave the lonelier

FATHER   A two two in English wit, a third in trite philosophy! Why is she always so contrary, Mother?

MOTHER   Why do you want to stay, Chrissy?

FATHER   Always the plug hole of attention?

MOTHER   Huw

FATHER   This is Lizzy's day, Mother, she should respect it

WOMAN   Chrissy can do as she likes

FATHER   Chrissy always does, doesn't she

WOMAN   The train's about to leave, Mama. I want to get off this mountain

MOTHER I know Lizzy

SISTER Leave me, I'll be fine on my own

MOTHER Chrissy, please

FATHER Less than twenty four hours home and she's firing on four cylinders of selfishness. God knows who she takes after!

MOTHER I wonder... Apologise to her, Huw

FATHER More point in a circle, Mother? Waste your breath if you have to

MOTHER JOINS CHRISSY. FATHER GOES TO LIZZY

MOTHER Chrissy...

SISTER You ask me why I don't come home

MOTHER Ignore your father, he doesn't mean half he says

SISTER It's the half he means that kills

MOTHER Let his words wash over you

SISTER I try to but...Why does he always pick on me, Mama? Why doesn't he ever pick on Lizzy? Why am I the Magdalen when she's the Virgin bloody Mary?

MOTHER Oh Chrissy

SISTER   I'm sick of it, sick to the back teeth of it. Do you remember when I was about eight? Dada gave Lizzy a book

MOTHER   A book?

SISTER   Yeah, a book he said she'd appreciate, assuming I wouldn't. It was the first time he drew a distinction between us. The next day, he brought me a book, prompted by his guilt; a gift he hadn't thought about, a gift so that I wouldn't feel left out; a gift too late. That's the story of my life, Mama. I've always been an afterthought

MOTHER   You haven't

SISTER   A p.s. daughter scrawled after the kisses have been exhausted

MOTHER   That's not true, Chrissy ... I remember that book. Your father bought it for Lizzy when she was very ill in hospital. We nearly lost her, Chrissy. She almost died, you could've grown up alone

SISTER   It might've been a blessing

MOTHER   Don't say that

SISTER   Not that I wish Lizzy dead, Mama... just missing; not from life, just from me. Because of her, I've always felt as if I've had to fight for love, Mama. I've fought for it and fought against it because I can't trust it. I can never work out whether I'm the object of devotion or the substitute for the real thing. That's the curse of being a twin; it's the ghosting of a person through constant competition.

MOTHER Chrissy fach...

BEAT

SISTER Alex was my boyfriend, Mama

MOTHER Yours?

SISTER Mine... At first he loved me, the way we should all be loved; Eves in our own Edens. It was three months before I told him I had a sister, five before I told him I was a twin. Then he had to see her. He insisted that we visit Lizzy in Aber so that he could contrast and compare. There's a strange irony in the air, don't you think; a Siberian nip in the Summer. It could quite easily be my baby flying the wind, Mama, but it isn't. It's Lizzy's, and that chills me, Mama, chills me dead.

FATHER Mother!

MOTHER God calls

SISTER Please don't tell Dada

MOTHER Not telling Dada is what I do best

SISTER I need time alone

MOTHER I've only ever been alone with the ironing

A MOMENT

MOTHER Think away from the edge, Chrissy. Thoughts can

sometimes lose your footing

SISTER   Don't worry

MOTHER Worrying's my stock in trade

FATHER   The train!

MOTHER I don't want to leave you here alone

SISTER   Here's best

MOTHER You were always my favourite, Chrissy...

SISTER   You don't have to say that

MOTHER I love your spirit

THEY EMBRACE

MOTHER As long as you're happy

SISTER   I will be

FATHER   Last call, Mother!

SISTER   The fat controller has spoken

MOTHER, FATHER AND WOMAN TRAVEL DOWN THE MOUNTAIN AND ON TO THE SEA LEAVING SISTER ALONE

SISTER   'Don't drive me North' you insisted when I picked you up from the airport, 'Drive me West . I want to walk where his feet'll never tread, map the geography he'll never inherit'

MAN   Lie on the spot where a cow died one night, follow the blood trail of a mouse who chewed through his own leg and dig up the shoe box grave of the squirrel that kissed a headlight. I know where the stinkhorn grows, the otter barks, the nuthatch walks and the Blue Heron nests. Take me to the land of memories never to be created in the mind of a baby, take me to a landscape lost.

SISTER   That night, after mapping exteriors, you charted interiors with your tongue, you called me Lizzy. Do you remember? I'm not sure whether you noticed your mistake. 'Come for me, Lizzy, just come' you said, cradling the small of my back with your palm. You cried as I came, your tears mingling with my pleasure, both of us shaking.
Lying back in my sister's bed, your stubble velcro'd to my crotch, I kept thinking about the anorexic twins, and the one who died so that the other could live.
'Have you ever called Lizzy my name by mistake?' I asked. 'Once' you said kissing the mole above my left thigh.
It was my turn to cry, female tears that run internally so that a man doesn't suspect a thing. I wanted you. I wanted to tattoo your flesh with my nails, but I was a twin and that meant you would always call me by her name and her by mine.
When we were kids, we used to play tricks on people. One of us would pretend to be the other and no-one would ever know the difference. Lying in Lizzy's bed, listening to the Blue Herons in the beech trees crying for a dead child, I realised that I never wanted to be mistaken for my sister again... especially when I'm

coming. 'Chrissy...' you began, ironing my thigh with the palm of your hand, I put my hand to your mouth 'Sh, just say nothing'
The next morning we drove north. Around Aber you told me that I was your favourite twin; always the competition! You listed our pros and cons as if you were comparing two cars of the same make you'd once driven. Apparently I had the best body and best suspension, but, however good the ride, we could never fuck again. 'We must think of Lizzy' you said, 'What if Lizzy ever found out, my life would be hell' Poor Princess Prissy in her crystal cita - fucking - del. Silly me, to think that I could ever compete with her 'immortal womb', the vehicle that carries your wildest ambition. I am just convenience Chrissy, the carbon copy; sad sod Chrissy, the one you fuck when the original is missing!

PAUSE

Last night you called me Lizzy again! Your apology was worse than had you said nothing; your embarrassment betrayed your emotion, it was obvious that you would've preferred to have been fucking the mirror's reflection. Well, it's high time for this glass to shatter and kill the twin.
I want to feel alone, alone not lonely. Happy within myself, missing nothing, just me for one glorious non fucking moment... I want to be... without comparison

AS SHE JUMPS OFF THE CLIFF'S EDGE, THE MAN GRABS HER BY THE ARM

MAN   Got you!

SISTER   Bastard!

MAN   Don't move

SISTER   Let me go !

MAN   Stay still

SISTER   I said let me go!

MAN   Hold tight

SISTER   Are you deaf?

MAN   What?

SISTER   Oh for God's sake...

MAN   I've just saved your life...

SISTER   So what?

MAN   So what!

SISTER   So what do you want?

MAN   Nothing

SISTER   Good, then I'll be off

MAN   Wait!

SISTER   Can't

MAN   Have you made a will?

SISTER   A what?

MAN   A last will and testament

SISTER   No, I haven't

MAN   That's bad

SISTER   I couldn't give a shit

MAN   What are you going to leave your mother?

SISTER   My mother!

MAN   What are you going to leave her?

SISTER   I can't believe this

MAN   Well?

SISTER   I haven't thought about it

MAN   Tell me and I'll let you go

SISTER   Are you real?

MAN   What are you going to leave her?

SISTER   My mother...

MAN   Tell me

SISTER   Oh God...I don't have much to give ... but..pain, I guess

MAN   And your father?

SISTER   You only said mother...

MAN   Your father?

SISTER   I don't know... Shame

MAN   And your sister?

SISTER   Freedom

MAN   And what will you leave me?

SISTER   Typical bloody man

MAN   What will you leave me?

SISTER   Realisation...

SHE BITES HIS HAND.

MAN   God!

HE LETS GO OF HER AND SHE DROPS TO HER DEATH. BY NOW, THE FAMILY ARE AT THE SEA SHORE. THE WOMAN SHIVERS

MOTHER   What's wrong, Lizzy?

WOMAN   Suddenly I feel so lonely

MAN   A family clenches in a crisis, like a fist around a magician's coin; holding nothing, sensing the emptiness, yet hoping, always hoping that it'll beat the magician, whilst knowing, knowing for a dead cert that it never will; such is the illusion of possession burning a hole in a tight fist.

FATHER   How are your legs, Mother?

MOTHER   Sorry?

FATHER   Your legs?

MOTHER   Disappointing

FATHER   Then the sea air'll do them good. As Nain used to say, 'If I could bottle it, I'd make a fortune'

MOTHER   She did

FATHER   Nain loved her sea, didn't she? She swore by it

MOTHER   Yes, Huw

FATHER   'Take me to the sea' she used to say, 'Take me to me to the sea, Huw bach. I feel a healing coming on'. That's what your Nain used to say, Lizzy

WOMAN   (IN A WORLD OF HER OWN) Did she?

FATHER   Do you remember her saying that, Mother?

MOTHER   I can hear her voice

FATHER   And I can picture her, dressed in her Sunday best, sitting in the passenger seat of our old Ford Anglia as if it was only yesterday. Do you remember?

MOTHER (WITH IRONY) It was bumpy in the back

FATHER Ah, but it was worth it, wasn't it? Just to see her rejuvenate with each breath of fresh sea air she'd take

MOTHER It was a miracle

FATHER A miracle, yes. It was, a miracle. That old Ford Anglia was indeed a chariot of the gods. That's why it was a such a shame when we part exchanged it, wasn't it, because Nain immediately took against the Hillman Minx, didn't she, Mother?

MOTHER I liked it

FATHER Oh, it was a lovely car, but it had an unfortunate name, Nain hated it, it went against her grain to be driven round in a Jezebel. I tried to explain, what's in a name, but she was having none of it...Poor Nain... I still miss our Sunday trips

MOTHER Every month of Sundays has to end, Huw

FATHER And all Ford Anglias rust to bits. I know that, Mother, but it doesn't make the memory easier to digest

MOTHER No, it doesn't

FATHER Then perhaps the sea air'll do us both a world of good

MOTHER Perhaps it will

WOMAN CARESSES HER STOMACH

MOTHER Are you all right, Lizzy?

WOMAN I'm all pain, Mama. At least my baby died without suffering, eh? He didn't linger like the poor kids in Ormond Street, bald and puffed up with drugs and dignity. He died like a baby James Dean - the beautiful corpse of a beautiful baby. He died quickly...clinically. I should be grateful, I guess, but a loss is a loss is a loss is a loss... and losses are felt by the living. Not that I've felt alive since the crash. Sleep and wake have merged to the point that I can't tell whether I'm dead or dreaming, Mama. I look at my arm and think, is this my arm? I look at you and think, are you my mother? I look at a cot in the corner of a room, and I think is my baby in there? Are you in there, my little Chubba? Mama sy' 'ma. Slowly I creep up to the cot to check that the world is not as perverse as it seems... Look in, and realise that it is. It really is... and much much worse than you ever said or I ever imagined

MOTHER Oh Lizzy fach...

WOMAN It's not your fault, Mama

MOTHER Don't cry

WOMAN I wish you could cry for me

MOTHER I do...

WOMAN No baby should die before its mother

MOTHER I know

WOMAN Take me home, Mama. I want to walk through the

> door and see my little baby crawl to greet me. I want to pick him up and press him close, feel his racing heart outpace mine. Take me home again, Mama. Take me back to yesterday. This isn't my life

MOTHER You are life, Lizzy

WOMAN I'm dead, Mama

MOTHER Don't say that

WOMAN Dead as Dadcu... You know, the only time I've felt alive since the crash was in a cheap hotel in Cardiff. I stayed there with Alex the weekend I lied to you about where I was going

MOTHER We knew where you had been

WOMAN I needed to see him, test the waters of futility. We were supposed to stay with Chrissy, but Chrissy turned prissy as she sometimes does, so after the pubs closed, we trawled Roath for a bed and breakfast.
We found a vacancy in a purple paradise, we climbed two flights to the attic, stripped naked as the light bulb and generated static between the sheets. And as we danced, I began to warm to the prospect of living again; a precious moments of healing.
Then he came and shattered the illusion. I didn't mind that we were out of sync, he did; synchronicity was always the be all and end all for him. Knowing that, I apologised, he accepted, but as he arched, I felt revenge pumping in, revenge and the re-appropriation of the hole through which his child had been born.

MOTHER God...

WOMAN   I was plugged with hatred, Mama. Up until then, we'd only ever made love, but lying next to him, staring at the flock wallpaper peeling, I felt as if I had just been raped by Peter fucking Pan. Oh I'm sorry Mama...

MOTHER   ... No, it's good to get things off your chest

WOMAN   I feel like a 38 triple D, I carry so much pain with me

PAUSE

WOMAN   The next morning he left early after settling the bill. I couldn't face breakfast alone, so I dressed and left soon after him. I glided along City Road towards town; numbed and invisible, I felt nothing. I was dead, Mama, dead to the world, and dead to the irony that inside this corpse, his eternal sperm were swimming

MOTHER   Lizzy fach

WOMAN   I'm an egg shell woman waiting to crack open, Mama. What sort of life can the dead offer the living?

MOTHER   You are alive. You must learn to accept, Lizzy. Accept for your sake and for the sake of your little baby. You have been given another chance, grasp it, please God, grasp it, Lizzy, or else nothing makes sense

THEY EMBRACE

WOMAN   Oh, Mama... Who do you blame for the accident?

MOTHER   God knows

WOMAN   But in your heart of hearts?

FATHER   Mother!

MOTHER   Yes, Huw?

FATHER   Shall we conclude this sad affair?

MOTHER   Of course, Huw

WOMAN   Mama, I don't want to do this

FATHER   Come on, Lizzy!

WOMAN   Please, Mama, I can't face it

MOTHER   It might help the pain

WOMAN   If it was me in that urn, how would you feel?

FATHER   Time's getting on

PAUSE

MOTHER   I'll have a word with him

FATHER   Time waits for no man, but man always waits for woman; why is that the eternal paradox?

MOTHER   It's merely one of them, Huw

FATHER   What about Lizzy?

MOTHER   Lizzy isn't up to it

FATHER   This ceremony is for her benefit

MOTHER   She doesn't see it like that

FATHER   It's her child in this urn

MOTHER   That's the point, Huw

FATHER   We're all upset, Mother. Believe me, I know how she feels

MOTHER   I doubt that

FATHER   This is hard for us all, mother

MOTHER   Put yourself in Lizzy's shoes, Huw

FATHER   Mother, I am wearing them. Lizzy? Lizzy fach...

WOMAN   I'm sorry, Dada...

FATHER   What's the matter?

WOMAN   This is too much for me

FATHER   I know you're upset, Lizzy, we all are; we care for you. That's why we must say our goodbyes together

WOMAN   What about Chrissy?

FATHER   Chrissy has dug an indecent grave... let her lie in it

MOTHER   Chrissy's your daughter, Huw

FATHER   She is dead to the day as far as I'm concerned. Let's just forget about her, and get on with the scattering

WOMAN   If you don't mind, Dada, I'll say my goodbyes alone

FATHER   I don't mind, Lizzy, but the dead might

MOTHER   For the sake of the living, Huw

FATHER   No Mother, this is important... both to me and my family

MOTHER   Huw, we are your family, and we're begging you. Why don't we scatter the ashes and leave Lizzy alone with the memory?

FATHER   That would be wrong, Mother. Lizzy is making a mistake she'll regret.

WOMAN   Please...

FATHER   Lizzy, we are damned as it is. Our lives have been cursed from the day that devil darkened our doorstep, don't compound our tragedy

MOTHER   For God's sake, Huw

FATHER   As God is my witness, Mother. We wouldn't be standing here about to scatter our sorrows upon the waves, were it not for him. Without him, we would have no sorrows to scatter

MOTHER   Oh, I think we could find some

FATHER   Meaning what, Mother?

MOTHER   Let's go home, Huw

FATHER   No, no. Meaning what?

MOTHER   Not now, Huw...

FATHER   What sorrows do we have to pull out of cupboards and dust down

WOMAN   Please, Dada...

FATHER   I have asked your mother a question, Lizzy. What sorrows?

MOTHER   This is neither the time nor the place, Huw

FATHER   It never is, is it, Mother? Blame hangs in our silence, like a shot songbird, well it's about time someone sang its lament...

MOTHER   ...don't, Huw...

FATHER   ...and now feels as good a time as any to sing

MOTHER   Oh God...

FATHER   For twenty-one years, I'd been composing a sweet air upon my heart's strings, a simple tune that would be my prize for all the worry and the pain; the final note of which would only be sung when I could give you to another man in holy matrimony

WOMAN   What a gift!

FATHER   Let me speak, Lizzy. When I'm finished, you can say your say. When the devil told me that you were pregnant, as if he was telling me the time of the next Cardiff - Chester train, I lost the tune.

Of course, I never expected you to remain pure until the altar, the twentieth century hasn't entirely passed me by, has it, Mother? But I believe that we should conduct our lives according to a divine score. However, I can't blame you for improvising, I blame only the beast that took a perfect air and sullied it; all that was beautiful became ugly. All that was Mozart became a cacophony.
And this poor little thing, whose remains lie in this urn, is the most discordant key in this dreadful Stockhausian symphony. The further away the sea carries our tragedy, the better

HE SCATTERS THE ASHES

MOTHER You are talking about your grandchild...

FATHER An unfortunate accident

WOMAN Please, Dada

FATHER A dreadful mistake

WOMAN He wasn't

FATHER Not unplanned but improvident

WOMAN That's not true, Dada!

FATHER That cat's eye was merely God's way of restoring the harmony.

WOMAN Sod God

FATHER Lizzy!

WOMAN   Sod him to hell!

FATHER RAISES HIS HAND

FATHER   Wash your mouth out!

MOTHER You can be so cruel, Huw

FATHER   To be kind, Mother, to be kind

MOTHER Apologise to your daughter

FATHER   She should apologise to me for bringing that bastard maker into our family.

WOMAN   Stop it, Dada

FATHER   A bastard maker; the root of our misery

MOTHER Don't, Huw!

FATHER   I accuse the devil incarnate

MOTHER So we're pointing fingers are we, Huw?

FATHER   Without the devil there is no fault

MOTHER Somehow, I doubt that

FATHER   I should've obeyed my instinct and let the dog rip his throat out when I had the chance
MOTHER Please, Huw?

FATHER   Mari hated him from the start

MOTHER   The dog hates everyone

FATHER   She sensed the evil within

MOTHER   For God's sake!

FATHER   For his sake I should've put a stop before the starting. For that I am guilty, I guess, but that is my only guilt

MOTHER   So you're a saint are you, Huw?

FATHER   He stole perfection and returned damaged goods; my little baby was violated!

WOMAN   How can you Dada?

FATHER   I am your father

MOTHER   Huw!

FATHER   Death demands its post mortem, Mother. Someone's responsible for this mess. If not him, then who?

BEAT

FATHER   Who, Mother?

MOTHER   Don't push me, Huw

FATHER   Who carries the can?

MOTHER   I don't want to blame

FATHER   Tragedies don't just happen. There are reasons...

MOTHER Leave it, Huw

FATHER Tell us. Who?

MOTHER For God's sake...

FATHER Mother...

MOTHER What do you want me to say?

FATHER I want you to back me up in this matter. Say the truth...

MOTHER The truth!

BEAT

FATHER Well ?

MOTHER The truth....After the crash, lying in a hospital bed, I blamed the world. I invented pedigrees of accusation, strings of conspiracy that linked everyone and everything. Inevitably, all lines led back to God, the natural scapegoat, and much easier to blame than your precious truth...
The doctors told me that if just one small bit of the blood clot had dislodged itself and made its way to my heart, I would've died. I lay awake in the ward at night and I'd pray that my legs wouldn't fail me

FATHER Thank God, you're alive

MOTHER Kept alive to blame. On a good day I could blame a saint and damn him; blame the driver of the oncoming car, blame the cats' eye manufacturer ... I could even blame you, Huw

FATHER   Me!

MOTHER   You, Huw... You... You were the one driving

FATHER   You were the one who wanted to stop

MOTHER   You chose to turn when you did

FATHER   Only because...

MOTHER   ... 'Because', never unspilt the milk, Huw, 'because', never sweetened a tragedy. That's why I prayed for one small clot to break free and stop my heart; one small clot that would stop the finger pointing. Because blame doesn't bring the dead to life again, Huw, it fossilises them in pain when their spirits should be soaring.

FATHER   Blame makes the loss bearable, Mother

MOTHER   Blame is a pointless party game, pinning the tail on a tragedy when all the guests have been and gone. No one's watching you, Huw, noone cares but still you carry on playing because you need to pin the failure upon someone. Well, stick the pin in your own backside, you have no right to blame anyone but yourself, none of us do. Our regrets and despairs are Calcuttas in our own hearts, we can't blank them out and forget about them, they form us and shape our suffering. We must deal with the pain as best we can, confront our guilt head on and stop blaming others, Huw. Because blame is a killer and blame kills the living... I blame myself

FATHER   Oh Mother, don't blame yourself

MOTHER   I blame myself for my silence when I should've spoken. The countless times you've put me down...

FATHER   When?

MOTHER   When have you not? You do it without realising, but that's nothing compared to the moments I sensed the tragedy yet said nothing. I kept silent for the sake of the twins, but I should've said something.... I should've said something so many times, but what's the point of speaking to someone who's not listening? So many silences wasted for nothing... for nothing, Huw. Perhaps, this day of truths, one silence should be broken.

FATHER   Mother...

MOTHER   Don't. The day of the crash, before driving to Lizzy's to pick up both her and her baby, you turned to me, and do you remember what you said...

FATHER   ...Is this relevant?

MOTHER   ... Pulling your gloves over your fingers that love to point, do you remember?

FATHER   No

MOTHER   You turned to me and said 'From today, I have a son'... my womb shrivelled with humiliation; my vagina closed and my breasts flattened. You had de-sexed me with a few unwitting words not meant to offend. That's what got me, the fact that you didn't

realise the impact of what you had said; it was just
another statement that rolled off your tongue,
unchallenged by a silent woman.
Silences can accuse, they can sometimes kill, but
silences to you are merely gaps to be plugged in a one
way conversation. 'From today, I have a son' you said

THE WOMAN COLLECTS STONES, PLACES
THEM IN HER DRESS, PICKS UP THE URN
AND WALKS INTO THE SEA

Let's go get him'
I have never wanted to hurt you, but I've wanted to
kill you many times, Huw; never more so than on that
journey between the North and the West. Sitting next
to you I prayed for a crash to carry us away before we
arrived at Lizzy's; before you could make a victim of
another generation. But that day, your God must've
been busy because he answered my prayer a touch too
late; the wrong life was taken on the wrong journey

MOTHER Who knows where tragedies really begin, mm? Perhaps
ours began with my silent prayer, or perhaps it had
begun earlier without us realising. There again,
perhaps our whole lives have been a tragedy waiting to
happen

SHE SINKS INTO THE SEA, THEN BOBS

FATHER You've had your say, Mother

MOTHER Sh! Huw!

FATHER Turn round and walk towards the shore

MOTHER It's too late

FATHER Please, Mother

MOTHER It's time to scatter our sorrows upon the waves

FATHER Mother, you'll catch your death

MOTHER BOBS AGAIN

MOTHER Death'll cradle me

WOMAN Mama!

MOTHER Live for me, Lizzy!

SHE SINKS

FATHER Mother!

WOMAN Mama!

FATHER Oh my God... I can't swim? Lizzy?

WOMAN Not in this condition

FATHER Nain thought that I'd drown, so I never learnt. I can't ride a bicycle either

WOMAN Mama!

FATHER Neither can your mother. It was one of the things we had in common when we first met

WOMAN For God's sake, get some help, Dada

FATHER It's late, there's no one around

WOMAN Find someone

FATHER Where?

WOMAN The village

FATHER She'll be drowned by the time I return

WOMAN She's going to drown anyway

FATHER But I want to be here with her

WOMAN Please, Dada

FATHER We've always been together

THE MAN REACHES AN ARM INTO THE SEA. THE MOTHER'S ARM BREAKS THE SURFACE

WOMAN There she is!

FATHER Mother! Take the stones out of your pockets, it'll help you float! Mother! Take the stones out of your pockets ...

WOMAN She can't hear you...

FATHER ...She's not listening. Mother, listen to me. Please, Mother, listen to me one last time and then I'll shut up and let you speak forever. Take the stones out of your pockets and turn back. Live, for God's sake, live! Mother! Suicide is a sin!

MOTHER And also salvation!

FATHER   A waste, whatever it is. For God's sake, Mother, listen. I just want to say, your silences were golden, commas and semi-colons in our conversation. I was listening, believe you me, I was listening to each mute moment, but silence has always made me edgy ... unnerved me. Speak to me. Say something... Gwenda! Don't leave me alone to spout monologues in a vacuum

WOMAN   Just go and get help, Dada

FATHER   What?

WOMAN   Help!

FATHER   Yes... of course. You stay here, just talk to her... No, listen to her... I'll take the car

FATHER   Mother! I'm going to get help!

WOMAN   She's waving Dada

FATHER   Stay with us, Mother! I won't be long...

FATHER DRIVES OFF

MAN   They're calling you

MOTHER   They can call me 'til kingdom come

WOMAN   Mama!

MAN   She sounds upset

MOTHER   Better this way, now that words have been spoken

WOMAN   Mama! Mama, please! Please, Mama!

MAN   This is embarrassing

MOTHER I've sat through more embarrassing silences than this; napalm silences that burn the flesh off a conversation, treacly silences that sweetly suffocate, bluebell silences that deaden the senses, and silences, so full of hate, they screamed.

WOMAN   Mama!

MOTHER My daughter screams for me

MAN   Lizzy

MOTHER You know her?

MAN   In passing

MOTHER Really. Do you know she's pregnant?

MAN   Yes

MOTHER Her second child?

MAN   I know

MOTHER Do you know the child's father?

MAN   Alex

MOTHER It's a small, small world, isn't it? My husband always hated Alex, his accent didn't fit. Before him, Lizzy'd been courting a boy called Gwion; a good boy, with a good Welsh name. His credentials were eisteddfodic, my husband approved of him. Gwion was to be the recipient of Huw's greatest gift, until Alex came along and stole it. I'm sorry, is this of interest to you?

MAN No, no, I'm listening

THEY SHARE A SMILE.

MOTHER A week or two after we found out that Lizzy was pregnant for the second time, Huw insisted we drove to Gwion's parents. You see, after our children had parted company, we kept in touch with the Wynnes, that's double 'n' 'e'; they were our sort of people I guess; Daniel Owen on the book shelf, caravans in August. Huw made out that we were passing through, but, in truth, ours was far from an innocent visit. Polishing off a Welsh cake, and without shame, Huw came straight to the point. He asked whether they could persuade their son to marry Lizzy and make a decent woman of her, even though she was carrying another man's baby. He honestly thought that they would consider his offer and straight-jacket their son into a double-barrelled wedding! Well, perhaps he had no shame, but the shame was mine... all mine.
The silence that followed his request hung in the air like a nerve gas, paralysing us, freezing the disbelief upon the Wynne's faces and the inane optimism upon Huw's.
'You must give me your recipe for Welsh cakes' I interrupted from the bottomless pit of my embarrassment. 'It's your recipe' Mrs Wynne replied, deepening it. I've been tumbling down into the darkness ever since

MAN   Let me pull you out

MOTHER That's very kind of you, but no thanks

MAN   I could pull you into the light

MOTHER There is light and there is light, and sometimes light shines in the darkness but, to be honest, I've always squinted in the sun. I'd be grateful if you'd let go of my hand

MAN   You're sure?

MOTHER Certain...It would've been nice to have met you

MAN NODS HIS HEAD. HE LETS GO OF HER HAND

MOTHER Thank you

SHE DROPS FOR THE FINAL TIME INTO THE SEA

WOMAN Mama!

WOMAN'S TEARS STAIN THE SANDS

WOMAN CLENCHES HER STOMACH

WOMAN Oh no, not now... Oh my God, another contraction...

THE FATHER IS DRIVING A CAR. DURING THE SPEECH, THE MAN GRADUALLY ENTERS THE CONVERSATION

FATHER Why the hell did you blame yourself, Mother? You shouldn't have done that, self-blame leads to insanity, what's the point of walking that route... especially with your nerves as they are, you know what you're like after the accident... your constitution's shot. Damn you, Mother! To die when I'm on the verge of retirement!

WOMAN   Mama!

FATHER   I never asked for the true truth, Mother. I never asked for that. I asked for the truth that blames a bastard whether he's guilty or not. Bastards are there to be sacrificed for the greater good. We can blame them with impunity, because we are the just, they are wrong, simple as that

WOMAN   Oh God! Chrissy!

FATHER   Not that I have any doubts about the devil incarnate, I'd have no qualms about donning the black handkerchief and damning him. I knew I shouldn't have welcomed him into my house. He breezed in, disturbing the comfortable cobwebs that caress the objets d'art of our history, re-defining our family in his terms. How dare he! And to think I had the grace to warn him against holding out his hand, because Mari would nip thinking she was about to be hit. I wish I hadn't. I wish I'd encouraged him to reach out and stroke the bitch, then sympathised as the vice clamped around his wrist. But it wouldn't have been Christian to take pleasure from other people's pain, even the devil's, so I turned the other cheek. Even when he announced Lizzy was pregnant and declared his undying love for her because the oral sex was good. You don't know that do you, Mother? That's a cross I've borne alone, even then, I turned the other cheek and bit my tongue. Bastard as he is! He taunted me with the impotency of fatherhood. He showed me the Grail then laughed because he knew I would never drink of it. No man has the right to do that. No man has the right to bait a father with his daughter's vagina then lick it!

AN UNDYING EXCLAMATION FROM WOMAN

FATHER Point your finger and live, Mother! Live! Don't you remember when Lizzy was taken ill during her pregnancy, the animal didn't even have the grace to phone us. Poor little Lizzy had to phone herself, her anaemic voice barely travelling the length of the wire home. Don't you remember we cried...dropped everything in our tears, then headed West.
He neglected her, Mother, my little Lizzy, he neglected her. Poor little thing lying in a white hospital bed; her skin, a grey November sky, her eyes, rain clouds on the horizon. Inside her, a little vampire was draining her life's blood. But it wasn't the child's fault, you can't blame the unborn who draw no distinction between sleep and wake, a foetus is blameless, it's the alive that violate.
Along the corridor he came, strutting his sex, boiling my blood. I walked towards him, honing my invective upon a blunt stone. 'I have one thing to say to you...' I began 'No, I have one thing to say to you' he cut in.

MAN Fuck off

FATHER The cheek

MAN The lip

FATHER The tongue

MAN   The emasculation

FATHER   The shame of it. The near dead clutched their bed pans out of embarrassment. But when he went to the Czech Republic, Mother... Oh yes, when he went to the Czech Republic on a cultural exchange, revenge was sweet. The look on his face as we pulled away with Lizzy and her little baby secure in the back seat of my car was worth all the pain and humiliation.
I would never have left you when our children were six weeks old, but there again, you were my wife...are my wife, please God. He refused to marry Lizzy on moral grounds; moral grounds, in God's name! It has always amazed me how the immoral can spout morality

MAN   Spout spout spout...

FATHER   The inanities of a hypocrite. He'd stolen my daughter, but I repossessed her and gained a son in the bargain. No way was I going to allow her to go back to him again. He desecrated beauty, but I resurrected it. That's why I feel no guilt for the accident, it was God's will and the devil's fault. The accident was, in essence, a blessing

MAN   A blessing

FATHER   Disaster gels... We'd read about it a week or so before, do you remember? It was a big story in a little paper. We were amazed by it. Acts of God are so fascinating. A cat's eye had become dislodged from the middle of a road, a car had run over it, popping it like a tiddlywink, and it shot through the windscreen of an oncoming car, killing the driver outright; poor man with his eyes on the road didn't see death coming

MAN   Poor blind man

FATHER   Of course, the chances of anything like that happening must be millions to one

MAN   But they happen

FATHER   God's grace is kaleidoscopic

MAN   Pain is infinite

FATHER   Mother spotted it first. 'Look' she said, pointing. I followed the line of her finger "My God". The chances of a second cat's eye becoming dislodged from its mounting must be...

MAN   Billions to one

FATHER   But there it was, left of centre, on the brow of a hill. A driver, unfamiliar with the road could have followed its course and careered into the ditch

MAN   Thank God you spotted it

FATHER   Isn't it odd how the fantastic happens when you least expect it, isn't it. Mind you, if the fantastic was commonplace then it wouldn't be fantastic, would it? 'We should stop in case there's an accident' Mother said, I agreed and pulled in

MAN   Just over the brow of an hill

FATHER   It was dark, there was nothing coming

MAN   How could you be so sure?

FATHER   The night was pitch, you could spot a car a mile off

MAN   And yet you still crashed?

FATHER   An unfortunate accident

MAN   Accidents can be avoided

FATHER   Not this one, this one was ordained. The narrow road dropped quite steeply after the brow. About fifty yards on the left, there was a turning into a field, so I decided to reverse in and drive back up to the top of the hill

MAN   For the sake of a few yards...

FATHER   It was wet, I didn't feel like walking. The turning was muddy. I had no trouble reversing but, as I pulled forward, my wheels span leaving the car vulnerably straddling the road. I stopped the engine to get out and assess the situation, I saw that I would have to reverse a bit and get another run at it. Getting back into the car, I was about to turn the ignition, when a boy racer, doing about sixty, sped over the brow of the hill. Perhaps at first he didn't see us, he kept coming... coming. Then I heard the scream of rubber attempting a purchase on a greasy road as we sat mesmerised by the inevitable disaster encroaching.

BEAT

FATHER   The point of impact was the back door on the driver's side. Behind it Lizzy's baby lay strapped in. The poor little angel slept through the collision... it never woke again

MAN   Sweet, sweet dreams

FATHER   The nightmares are mine. Had, had and had, but had the beast not decided to fly the nets of responsibility so soon after his son's birth, then we would not have been driving down that particular road at that particular moment, and that which happened would never have come to pass. It was the devil's design

MAN   But your execution

FATHER   What?

MAN   You were to blame?

FATHER   Not entirely

MAN   Not entirely?

FATHER   Blame is relative

MAN   Bollocks.

FATHER   I'm merely flesh and blood

MAN   Flesh tears, bones break

FATHER   To err is human

MAN   So plead absolution, nothing ventured nothing gained.. Take the blame for the death of a child who will never know his own name; a child who could have been someone... done something. One day, he could've stopped off for a piss in Pasadena, met a girl and married her. You could've been the great

grandfather of a future President of America; a child born to change the world; an astronaut or a gutter sweeper, a mercenary or a healer, he could've been anything as long as his death certificate didn't read, 'No name, Child of...'Child of what? Child of time? Child of no bloody time at all?
Can't you see what you've done? Not just the accident, but the lives you've ruined, the victims you've made, just because of your selfishness and fucking presumption!

FATHER I am only a man..

MAN I know..

FATHER ... a man born to crucify myself on the cross of my own making. I would've given my life to be a god but, God knows, I'm only human and humans are prey to the devil's hand. I made mistakes like the best of them

MAN PICKS UP THE CAT'S EYE

MAN If I had a heart, it'd bleed for you

FATHER For God's sake!

MAN Stop hiding behind him!

FATHER I know no other way to live. It's not easy being the rock when you're a mass of contradiction... To offer answers when you know nothing...To feel your dignity eroding and your sex diminishing

MAN Life's a shit.

FATHER   What's that?

MAN   Can you see it? Can you see the car coming in the opposite direction? See the cat's eye flipped and flayling? What are the chances of anything like this happening eh, a trillion to one? Improbable, but it's happening...

FATHER   Forgive me.

MAN   Was that a sorry?

FATHER   Yes!

MAN   Too late

THE CAT'S EYE SMASHES THROUGH THE CAR WINDSCREEN AND INTO THE FATHER'S FACE. AT THIS MOMENT THE WOMAN SCREAMS.

WOMAN   Mama!

THE DEAD MOTHER AND SISTER ASSIST AT THE BIRTH

SISTER   Dyna ei ben o (There's his head)

MOTHER   Ac eto (Once again)

SISTER   Gwthia, Lizzy (Push ,Lizzy)

WOMAN   Ffycin hel... Sori, Mama

MOTHER   Jyst gwthia wnei di (Will you just push)

SISTER   Ei sgwydda bach o (His little shoulders)

MOTHER Ma ar ei ffor', Arglwydd mae'n ddel (He's on his way, God he's beautiful)

SISTER Llond pen o wallt (A full head of hair)

MOTHER Dalia ati... Gwthiad bach efo... (Keep going... one more push)

WOMAN Oh, Mama...

MOTHER Gwerth y byd o boen? (Worth a world full of pain)

INTO THE WORLD

WOMAN A mwy na hyny (And more)

SISTER Caru ti, Lizzy (Love you, Lizzy)

WOMAN Oh, y peth bach. Mama, sy ma... gad i mi dy ddal di'n dynn dynn, teimla 'nghalon yn gysur i chdi
(oh, the small thing. It's Mama... Let me hold you close, feel my heart comforting you)

MOTHER Run ffunud â fo (The spit of him)

SISTER Del (Beautiful)

WOMAN Ontydi (Isn't he)

MOTHER Sgen ti enw iddo fo? (Have you got a name for him?)

WOMAN Phoenix

MOTHER Paid â son (Don't be so silly)

WOMAN   Dyna 'i enw fo. Phoenix Bach Griffiths (That's his name. Small Phoenix Griffiths)

MOTHER   Neno'r tad! (In the name of God!)

SISTER   Double barrelled?

WOMAN   Ddeiff na ddim byd double barrelled allan o' nghroth i (Nothing double barrelled come from my womb)

MOTHER   Ga'i ddal o? (May I hold him?)

WOMAN   Mae on grisial (He's crystal)

MOTHER HOLDS CHILD

MOTHER   Bysedd gwlan cotwm... Oh, ma'n gariad ontydi... (Cotton wool fingers.. He's a love, isn't he...)

MAN STANDS OVER THE FAMILY GROUP

MAN   It's me, little brother, the one who'll never brave the fears before you... Don't cry ? You've got a bit of ash in your eye, it's me, I think.... I'd wipe it away, but I can't touch you; not in that way, I'm sorry. Not that I'm to blame, no-one's to blame any more, but it's such a shame; the knees wwe could've scraped, the blood we could've spilt... but maybe it's for the best; no brother, no mud, no Avon bridge; no loss, no pain.

Beat

MAN   No, there's always pain, Fuck it...

HE RISES AND HOVERS SIX FEET ABOVE WALES

MAN I tell you what though, let's do a deal eh, litle brother; a deal between the hungry and the fading ? I'll look after you if you'll live for me. Live a life big enough for us both. And when you meet Dada... when you meet <u>our</u> Dada... shit..Shit's so complicated isn't it, not that you'd know yet, but you'll soon scent it...Oh, and by the way, in twenty years time when you pass through Pasedena, don't stop off for a piss, ok; keep going...just keep going...live...live, little brother...live, for both our sakes...

FADE TO TEARS

> hawlfraint/copyright IAN ROWLANDS
> 1st draft Annaghmakerrig 13.i.98
> (as rehearsed 8.v.98)
> 2nd draft Cyfforff Crewe 13.ii.99
> (as rehearsed 22.iii.99)

Blue Heron in the Womb. Liz Armon-Lloyd & Jonathan Nefydd

photo: Dave Daggers

FADE TO TEARS

The first thing I loved were these strange words: blue...heron...in the womb... Whatever it meant - it seemed strange, exotic, potent - a title for a myth or a fairy-tale - BLUE HERON IN THE WOMB.

Blue Heron in the Womb was first performed at the Tron Theatre, Glasgow the 21st May 1998 - that's what it states in the programme. I don't know when I got seduced by the mystery and rich darkness of the title, but I think it happened in the Tron Bar, where Ian Rowlands joined me for coffee during Theatr y Byd's triumphant Glasgow presentation of his *Marriage of Convenience*. It struck a chord in Glasgow. Identity, nationhood, language, tradition - all the old clichéd questions suddenly coming to life in a passionate monologue which filled the Tron stage with a multitude of Welsh characters, mountains, families, vistas - in the context of the distant and self-important royal nuptial solemnities. It struck a chord with the Glasgow audiences socially and politically, it struck a chord with me artistically. The directness of its imagery, the daring of its language, the simplicity of its staging - it was provocative, and angry - just the play for an August evening en route from the Edinburgh Festival.

Ian's passion and energy of vision were infectious as we chatted that afternoon in the bar. We talked theatre and we talked dreams. We both felt there had to be a future for a creative partnership between our two companies. That's when Ian uttered the magic words: Blue Heron in the Womb. I gasped at the beauty, before I realised the pain of those words...

Some months later, there was Ian again - script in hand - We were sitting across a desk in my temporary office. Ian offered to read a section of the partly written script - and off we went - with the two sisters, I think, talking on the mountain top: of sex and jealousy, death and hope. Intense, hugely emotional and linguistically so exquisite and precise...

Theatr y Byd returned to the Tron in March, Ian and his designer, Sean Crowley and the ubiquitous Dave Roxborough discussing, drawing, sketching, deeply focused, involved - the play acquiring its physical reality amidst the cups of capuccino.

It duly opened on May 21st. In the darkness I found myself plunged into the world of a Greek tragedy - or rather a Welsh tragedy of Greek dimensions ! A male figure seemed to be hovering in the shadows of the scenes - he never seemed to touch the ground. A woman was helping an older man get dressed. Two young women did the ironing. The older man was quite still on a small raked platform in the middle of the stage, the women revolving around him. Some kind of a sphinx glimmering on some kind of a backdrop. It begins.

The mirrors of language and images, the counter-point of words and actions - it was an unforgettable journey through this beautiful, powerful and relentless myth of death and rebirth. As a new child was born, and an old language was spoken, the audience, as if on cue, followed what I later discovered to be the final stage-direction in the script: FADE TO TEARS. So we did.

Irina Brown
Artistic Director
Tron Theatre
Glasgow

Love in Plastic

Love in Plastic was first performed at the Glynn Vivian Gallery, Swansea on the 25th of May 1995 with the following cast:

MAN   **Jonathan Nefydd**
WAITER **Brian Hibbard**
WOMAN   **Helen Griffin**
AGENT   **Wynford Ellis Owen**

director   **Ian Rowlands**
technical manager/lighting designer   **David Roxburgh**
stage manager   **Ruth Llywelyn**
costume design   **Mein Roberts**
original music   **Robin Williamson/Lawson Dando**

production manager **Dafydd Wyn Roberts**
administration   **Angharad Jones**

The performance took place within an art installation created by Tim Davies and commissioned with the assistance of the Arts Council of Wales.

LOVE IN PLASTIC

The lights come up on an empty restaurant. The owner has a magnifying glass. He is looking for economic recovery.

WAITER Norr even a measly Glamorgan sausage. I ask ew. Where in hell's name's this economic recovery, I can't find it. I'd have more luck findin' ambishun in Swansea.

Phone rings.

He plays pre-recorded crowd atmos to give the impression that the restaurant is full. Harold enters dressed in a space suit.

WAITER Good evening... Welsh Rarebits, can I 'elp ew? Yes... Ye-es? Yewer sorry! I'm the one that should be sorry, I am sobbing bloody sorry. Here I am, a desperate man about to pawn a limb and yew cancel without warnin'. What right do yew have to sit at the end of yewer mohair phone and cancel yewer bookin'. Sorry pal, but I don't care who's dead! I garrow make a livin'...

Slams down the phone. Harold turns to go.

MAN I'll come back later.

WAITER Wha'! No no. Don't go!

MAN Are you closed?

WAITER Have you got any money?

MAN I've got plastic.

WAITER   For plastic I'd rip open my stomach and fry yew a kidney. 'Ow can I 'elp yew kid?

MAN   Am I in the right place?

WAITER   For years I've been wondering the same thing. But, right place or wrong place, yewer in my place; the only place to be in. Welcome to "Welsh Rarebits" – the best thing since mam's cookin'.

MAN   Sounds inviting…

WAITER   Tastes a treat, so pull up a pew.

MAN   I'd love to.

WAITER   So what's stopping ew 'en?

MAN   I'm not sure whether I've booked a table –

WAITER   Well that's easily sorted, lessava shifty, kid (*In book*) … I got a table in 'ere for seven thirty, name of Ebenezer?

MAN   No.

WAITER   There's a shame. Well not a shame really, I mean, I wouldn' inflict a name like Ebenezer on my worst enemy. With a name like Ebenezer yewd feel like a walkin' chapel wouldn' you. How about Bartholomew?

MAN   No.

WAITER   There's a pity. Ere's a biwt… Harold?

MAN   That's my name!

WAITER   Harold?

MAN   Yes, but everyone calls me Harry.

WAITER   Harry?

MAN   Yes, Harry Vernon Love-Jones.

WAITER   Is tharr eyephenated?

MAN   Yes.

WAITER   Well kiss my Aunt Fanny! Harry Vernon Love-Jones!

MAN   Vernon is my father's name, Love runs in my family.

WAITER   With a name like 'at!

MAN   So have I booked then?

WAITER   Yew are where yew should expect yewerself to be.

MAN   Good, I am glad.

WAITER   So am I kid. Right 'en, 'Arry Vernon, Love the hyphenation, Jones, let's get the pot cookin'. Would ew be smokin' or non smokin'?

MAN   Non smoking.

WAITER   There's hygienic. Personally, I smoke more than 'ot oil in a wok. I've tried to give up, but yew can't extinguish a smokin' non-smoker like me.

MAN   A non-smoking smoker?

WAITER It's to do with life cover. (*Nose tap*)

MAN   I see.

WAITER Seen but not 'erd, I 'ope.

MAN   Mum's the word.

WAITER Absoliwtlee. Now, how about this table over by yur?

MAN   That table?

WAITER Assawun.

MAN   I... I... I'm not sure

WAITER What do yew mean "yewer not sure"?

MAN   I'm not sure if it's the right one.

WAITER A table's a table, mun.

MAN   It's our first date! I want everything to be perfect!

WAITER So yew wannw make an impreshun do yew?

MAN   A big one.

WAITER Then forget the table. The A four seven O to a woman's affecshun is the company; listen to 'er, pretend yew understand 'er – that always makes 'em 'appy.

MAN   I'll bend both ears.

WAITER   Yew bend 'em good.

MAN   I'll pay attention.

WAITER   Yew pay for most things in this world son, but I'll tell ew this for free. If yew really wanna prick a woman's 'eart, there's nothin' more impressive than the social anabolic of money.

MAN   I think I've got enough.

WAITER   For yewer sake, I 'ope ew 'ave. Yew see kid, it's not wharrew pay, it's how yew pay it. So if yew wanna bowl an' roll this girl of yewers tonight, this is what I'd do if I was ew. After the meal, ask for the bill. Then when it comes don't even look at it, ignore it; as if it were a dead Tory or some'in'.

WAITER   Just drop yewer plastic nonchalantly on the table, then turn and give 'er a smile; as wide as if the bill was only two pounds fifty.

MAN   And that'll impress her?

WAITER   Not entirely.

MAN   Oh.

WAITER   Yew 'ave to leave a big tip as well.

MAN   How big?

WAITER   Thassa queschun an' an arf thar is. How big's a ball of string, how long's a perfect marriage?

MAN   I don't know.

WAITER   Precisely. Just ram yewer 'and into yewer pocket, pull out whatever's in there an' throw it on the table. Cause the bigger the tip the bigger the impression, the bigger the impression the bigger the woo an' the bigger the woo the better for yew.

MAN   I'll bear it in mind... if she ever turns up.

WAITER   (*As he exits*) She'll be 'ere, don't ew worry; late's 'er perogative kid....

Exit Waiter. Enter Woman pursued by Ego.

WOMAN   ...I have just had a Joan Collins of a journey, darling. Please, please accept my apologies. Will you ever be able to forgive me?

MAN   I've forgiven you already.

WOMAN   Are you sure you won't hate me forever?

MAN   I promise.

WOMAN   What a love you are. Kiss kiss... (*Kisses either side of his helmet, no contact*) God! This place is like a crypt.

MAN   It's pretty dead, isn't it?

WOMAN   Dead, darling! It's like Port Talbot.

MAN   It does lack a certain atmosphere.

WOMAN   It's as dead as God's toenails in here.

MAN   I'm sorry. Would you prefer to eat somewhere else?

WOMAN   Anywhere in mind?

MAN   Nowhere near.

WOMAN   The further away the better...

Enter Waiter.

WAITER Good evening, madam.

WOMAN   Damn...

MAN   ...We're caught...

WOMAN   ...Like flies on Vapona.

WAITER So yew found the right place 'en.

WOMAN   Is this the right place?

WAITER Apparently.

Man nods.

WOMAN   Oh God...

WAITER Here, let me take yewer coat?

WOMAN   No, no it's.... O....K!

It is off before she can protest.

MAN   Perhaps we'd better stay.

WOMAN   Do we have a choice?

WAITER   Should I 'ang yewer coat, madam?

WOMAN   Yes, but use a coat hanger, there's a love.

WAITER   I'll 'ang it as carefully as I would 'ang myself.

WOMAN   Yes, you do that.

Waiter exits.

WOMAN   God! If there's the minutest droop in his shoulders I think I shall sue him. Droopy shoulders are so unbecoming, don't you think so, darling?

MAN   I've never thought about it.

WOMAN   Take my word for it, they are about as sexy as big tits in the 'sixties, and I should know, it was a bloody nightmare decade for me. My tits don't sag, do they love?

MAN   Not that I've noticed.

WOMAN   Are you sure?

MAN   I haven't really looked.

WOMAN   Well look dear, look and tell me.

MAN   What can I say?

WOMAN   The truth love, the truth.

MAN   I don't think so.

WOMAN   What do you mean "you don't think so"?

MAN   They look perfect.

WOMAN   Perfect, really… Oh, what a darling word perfect is; such an appealing word to the flawed. Am I… truly perfect, darling?

MAN   As perfect as perfect can be.

WOMAN   Really? Am I beautiful then?

MAN   Truly beautiful.

WOMAN   Honest injun?

MAN   To me, you are the most beautiful woman in the world.

WOMAN   To you!

MAN   Yes.

WOMAN   What do you mean "to you"?

MAN   To me.

WOMAN   Aren't I the most beautiful woman in the world, full stop?

MAN   You are the most beautiful woman in the world…

probably.

WOMAN   Probably! What does that make me – a lager?

MAN   No, what I mean is that if everybody else in the world came to see you as I see you, and to think of you as I think of you, then you would probably be the most beautiful woman in the world to everybody.

WOMAN   Bugger reason, Harry, just flatter me.

Enter Waiter.

WAITER   May I seat ew, madam?

WOMAN   … If you have to.

WAITER   This is the wine list and this is the menu.

WOMAN   Thank you.

WAITER   The menu, sir.

MAN   N-no, not for me.

WAITER   Isn't sir 'ungry?

WOMAN   Aren't you hungry, darling?

MAN   I don't want anything to eat.

WAITER   Why not?

MAN   I don't eat.

WAITER   What!

WOMAN   He said he doesn't eat.

MAN   Or drink.

WAITER   What are ew, a dromedary?

MAN   Please don't misunderstand me.

WAITER   I'm strainin' veins tryin' not to.

MAN   Of course I eat and drink, but I only eat and drink at home, never when I'm out, never...

WAITER   ... in a restaurant...

MAN   No.

WAITER   ... where people ordinarily come to eat and drink...

MAN   No.

WAITER   ... and impress their friends by spending lots of money.

MAN   .... Sorry.

WAITER   Sorry don't ice my bun, kid! Sorry don't make an impreshun. Now warrabout madam?

WOMAN   Oh... I'm the queen of indecision.

WAITER   God's teeth, mun! Ave a think and I'll cum back later 'en.

WOMAN   No, no, that's unnecessary, I'll have a small side salad and a glass of water.

WAITER   A small side salad…

WOMAN   Yes.

WAITER   With wa'?

WOMAN   On its own.

WAITER   Yew can't 'ave a side salad on its own. A side salad is a salad to the side of a main dish; yew can't 'ave a side salad sitting beside itself, it's doolally tap mun. Do'n anything else tickle yewer fancy?

WOMAN   Darling, I have less appetite than a gassed canary.

WAITER   Oh God… Do you wan' yewer water, before the salad or after?

WOMAN   During, darling.

WAITER   My pleasure… Oi. Let me plant a friendly word in yewer yur kid. Bearing in mind the chat we had earlier, yewer performance so far wouldn't make an impreshun in butter. Yew wanna pot the ball and win the goldfish, don't ew kid?

MAN   Of course I do.

WAITER   Then beef the bill up a bit.

Waiter nods and exits.

WOMAN What a cheeky little git. He's as bad as the taxi driver I had on the way over here. Before I'd closed the door he'd slammed down the meter and hit warp factor ten… My make-up smudged with the G force, darling. And talk! He talked a gross to the dozen.
I cannot begin to describe how disembowellingly tedious his conversation was, and for the privilege of being bored rigid he charged me four pounds twenty. Four pounds bloody twenty, his life story wasn't even worth two p. Anyway I paid the exact fare because I was desperate to get away from the ghastly man, then I asked for a receipt – If I did.

MAN Did you?

WOMAN Of course I did, it's the obsession of my profession, darling. "People normally pay for their receipts, lurv" he said, without a hair on his tongue. The presumption! Then he clicked his fingers like an Oliver with lip, "You don't take a hint do you, lurv" he said. "What about the tip?" A tip! He expected a tip after boring me stupid? Right, I thought, enough's enough, I'm not suffering this git. So I stabbed him with my Opinel eyes and said, "Darling, you've been such a good driver, you deserve a big, big tip"; his eyes melted in his face like ashes in a plastic dustbin. "Give it to me, lurv," he said…
So I did, I looked the dog's dick in the face and said, "Here's my tip, darling," (*Poking a fig – middle finger thrust*)

MAN No!

WOMAN Damn right I did, then I turned and walked calmly towards this restaurant on the blue carpet of his abuse.

MAN   That is awful.

WOMAN   Would you believe it?

MAN   I believe it.

WOMAN   The baboon-arsed cheek of it! Like restaurants where it's written, "We do not include a gratuity" in bold print at the bottom of the menu. But leave without tipping and if looks could kill, they'd kill you.

The phone rings.

WOMAN   It probably said that on the menu for this place. Did you notice?

MAN   No.

WOMAN   Neither did I, but I bet it was there. This is the sort of place where there's no room to swing a cat but by God they'd find room to skin one.

The Waiter plays the pre-recorded 'atmosphere' before answering.

WAITER   Welsh Rarebits, can I 'elp ew? I'm sorry? What? I can't 'ear yew very well, we've got a bit of a crowd in tonight. Bear with me. Come on folks 'ave some feelings! I'm on the phone 'ere! (*Turns the radio down*) Thass better… Right 'en, where were we? Who? Should I know her? Oh… 'ang about, I'll see if she's 'ere.

He rests the receiver. He goes over to the woman.

WOMAN   …Like the set menu I once saw by the bahnhof in

Copenhagen – 'Homos, Lesbians and Animals'; I mean, who could turn down that bargain!

WAITER 'Scuse me buttin' in love, but is yewer name Isabel?

WOMAN Why?

WAITER Cause if it is there's a phone call for yew.

WOMAN Who is it?

WAITER I didn't ask, sorry.

WOMAN Oh God…

MAN What's wrong?

WOMAN Nothing hopefully, darling.

She goes over to the phone. Waiter sits next to Man.

WOMAN Hello… Hello… Hel-low? They've hung up.

WAITER Thass odd, there was only one of 'em.

WOMAN Was it a man or a woman?

WAITER He didn't let on.

WOMAN So it was a man, then? Did he happen to mention his name?

WAITER Not a dicky, love.

WOMAN Thanks…

WAITER   No trouble at all… so would you mind doing *me* a favour. On yewer way back would yew bring yewer side salad and water over, it's by the phone. My businessman's ankle playin' up again see; it always 'appens when I'm rushed off my feet.

WOMAN   Is this it?

WAITER   That's very kind of ew. (*To Man*) Remember, kid, the bigger the tip the bigger the impreshun, the bigger the impreshun the bigger the woo, the bigger the woo…

MAN   The better for me.

WAITER   The better for yew. (*To Woman*) Thanks a bunch, love. Ge' yewer nose in the troff 'en…

Exit Waiter.

WOMAN   Did you notice if cheek was chalked up on the board as special of the day; two insults for the price of one? Whatever happened to good old-fashioned decency? Deconstructed probably. If my grandfather was alive he'd turn in his grave. 'Good manners cost nothing,' he used to say, you probably have to pay for a please in this place.
My grandfather was a true gentleman; a paragon of civility; his blue blood runs in my veins, not your common or garden me. My grandfather was a White Russian.

MAN   Really.

WOMAN   Vraiment, darling. He fled Petrograd in 1917; Potemkin shot in and my grandfather shot out quicker

than ripe acne… He ended up in Paris where there was a large exile community. He was so 'pas un sou' as the French say, that he was reduced to working in a restaurant. Poor sod.
But even there he retained his dignity. He prided himself on being polite to all his customers; he had impeccable manners. It comes with good breeding. Do you know, in Paris he once shared a room with two Dukes who killed themselves gambling.

MAN　There's posh.

WOMAN　It's exotic, darling.

MAN　It's incredible.

WOMAN　Gospel true.

MAN　No…

WOMAN　Why should I lie? I've only just met you.

MAN　I believe you.

WOMAN　Good.

MAN　Cross my heart and hope to die.

WOMAN　Oh God…

MAN　What's wrong?

WOMAN　The truth is, darling… it's a bloody lie…

MAN　A lie?

WOMAN Yes. A big porky.

MAN You lied to me…

WOMAN A little white fibbie. Force of habit. I've never found the truth very seductive. Why live the truth when you can dream luxury? I'm an actress, darling, an actress who was reared in the Rhondda Valley.

MAN With a voice like that!

WOMAN My voice is my Passport to Pimlico; my professional lie. I am a professional liar, darling. I lie to survive and I've lied so long that I've forgotten the sound of sincerity. The truth is rarely sexy, I've never put much store in it; would you if you were brought up in Blaenllechau?
Would you own up to having been dragged up in a village that clings to the mountain like a viral pile? In Blaenllechau you had to lie to survive. Everybody lied, about everything, degrees of lying to keep sane.
The poorer you were the more you lied. I lied more than most, darling, so even as a kid it was obvious that I was going to make lying my living. And I did, and lying has allowed me to lead the sort of life that I always wanted.
The one drawback is that full-time lying is like a house in Trehafod, unless you've had a massive grant from the council to underpin it, at some point it's bound to go. You know what I mean?

MAN I know those houses.

WOMAN I thought you would. I knew you would… I don't know what it is about you, darling, but I have this feeling that I can talk with you, not talk at you or talk to you, but talk with you, and I feel that you'll listen to me.

MAN I will.

WOMAN Will you, darling? Will you really? Will you really co-pilot my flights of fancy?

MAN Yes.

WOMAN Mind you, most men listen, don't they: in through one ear then out through the other; a listening man is hardly a rare flower.

MAN I'm not like most men.

WOMAN So what separates you from the weeds, what makes you Chelsea, darling?

MAN My word.

WOMAN Your word! Words mean nothing, they are the currency of men. I should bloody know, I've surrounded myself long enough in them.
My words are irrelevant, the battle is the unravelling. Not that I hold out much hope of being understood or of understanding anyone.

MAN Why?

WOMAN I've been an actress too long to believe in communication.

MAN There must be hope.

WOMAN   Hardly any, especially during the Wednesday matinee.

MAN   A Wednesday matinée?

WOMAN   As dead as boxing day. So we might as well lie, because without any way of communicating a truth what's the point of speaking it. A lie is just as good, because both are equally invalid.

MAN   Do you always lie then ?

WOMAN   Only when I'm telling the truth.

MAN   So you lie about everything ?

WOMAN   Everything, darling.

MAN   Please don't lie to me.

WOMAN   Why ever not ?

MAN   Because your lies would kill me.

WOMAN   My god ! Once more, I'm floored by your sincerity. What are you like ?

MAN   What am I like ?

Enter Agent

WOMAN   You're too real to be true, Harry. So I'll be buggered if I can believe in you, and by the same chalk don't bloody believe in me.

AGENT   I believe in you, babe, I have no choice, I spend your money.

WOMAN   Oh God!

AGENT   Garrie Bright, theatrical agent to the stars.

WOMAN   Not now, I'm busy, Garrie.

AGENT   My dear Bella, if Tony Hopkins phoned me, here and now, here and now on this mobile phone…

WOMAN   Was it you that phoned earlier?

AGENT   … Don't block the flow, babe… And said, "Garrie Boy, there's a part that's tailor made for Isabel in my next film, I need her Garrie, I need her desperately, desperately! Can I have her?", would you want me to say, 'Not now, Tone, she's busy'?

WOMAN   No.

AGENT   So how busy is busy, Bella?

WOMAN   How urgent is urgent, Garrie?

AGENT   Well, I'd like to say that Wales has a National Theatre and you're its first star.

WOMAN   But it hasn't and I'm not.

AGENT   No, you're not… unfortunately. But some day your bath will shine, babe. Everybody in the bizz respects you. But you can't live on a percentage of respect. So listen up, baby, I am talking starring role, star-ring role in a tightly scripted soap opera to be screened several times nightly on network TV.

WOMAN Oh God. It's another advert for bath cleaner, isn't it?

AGENT Babe babe babe, some people would drink bleach to be half as successful as you. It may be just another detergent commercial, but it's 'good clean family entertainment' and it could appear on a bank balance near you. So think about it.

WOMAN No thanks.

AGENT Don't be thoughtless, babe, do it for my bank balance if not for yours. Think of how my fifteen percent will enrich my life and keep me in the style to which you've allowed me to become accustomed…

WOMAN Fifteen percent! I though it was twelve and a half –

AGENT Twelve and a half is art, love. Advertising is both the bath water and the baby. By letting me carve off fifteen percent it'll make you feel better for having sold out in the first place; I'll certainly feel better, people's kitchens will be cleaner and everybody will be happier. So what more could you want?

WOMAN A worthwhile career.

AGENT All good things come to those who wait.

WOMAN Darling, I have been waiting all my life; there's a limit to how far you can stick out your tits and make small talk with small men. I want a good theatre job, a period telly; an obscure Dickens or something. I want to do some work that will challenge me not scour me.

AGENT   I can relate to that, I can't understand it, but I can relate to it. But you see, babe, you can't afford to wait penniless in the dock 'til your artship comes in… So put your thinking cap on and see sense, babe.

WOMAN   If I agree to the audition will you go away?

AGENT   There is no audition, that's the beauty of it. You are now the doyen of detergent. The producer asked for you by name, by name! Now I know he's hardly a Hopkins, but he is a squit kid going places. 'Where's Isabel?' he said. 'What's her availability?' 'Oh, she's busy, very busy,' I said, playing hard to get. So he said, 'I want her whatever the cost,' and I said you'd be only too happy.

WOMAN   Well thanks for consulting me first.

AGENT   I'm your guardian angel babe, so aren't you going to thank old Garrie Bright?

WOMAN   Not tonight, Garrie. I'll call you at your office tomorrow morning…

AGENT   What about a quick celebratory drink?

WOMAN   No thanks.

AGENT   Come on.

WOMAN   I don't want one.

AGENT   That's not like you…

WOMAN   ...Do the decent thing, Garrie!

AGENT   Don't murder messengers, babe... So what's your friend's name then?

WOMAN   ...Harry...

AGENT   Harry what?

MAN   Harry Veron Love-Jones, pleased to meet you. *(He does not shake.)*

AGENT   Is that hyphenated?

MAN   Yes.

AGENT   Babe. Is it wise to be left alone with a spaceman with a hyphenated sexuality?

WOMAN   Garrie, darling, I'm perfectly safe...

AGENT   No one's perfectly safe these days.

WOMAN   For God's sake, Garrie go away! I'll pop in and talk to you tomorrow morning, but right now I'm in the middle of really interesting conversation, so I'd be grateful if you would just bugger off and play with your percentages! OK, darling?

Waiter enters.

WAITER Sir! Good evening. Are you with the party –

WOMAN   No he's not.

WAITER   Have you booked –

WOMAN   He was just going.

WAITER   Oh...

AGENT   Now, now, Isabel. We still live in a semblance of a democracy. I can eat where I want, and wherever I want if I'm hungry.

WOMAN   Please don't do this.

AGENT   And to be honest I'm starving, I barely stopped for lunch, I'm so busy. I haven't booked a table though... Does that pose a problem?

Agent gives Waiter a tenner.

WAITER   No problem arrol. It'll be a pleasure to scweeze ew in... Smokin' or non-smokin'?

AGENT   Non-smoking.

WAITER   There's 'ealthy. I smoke more than suspicious fires, me. I'm a smokin' non-smoker.

AGENT   A smoking non-smoker.

WAITER   It's to do with life cover.

AGENT   I see.

WAITER   Seen but not 'eard, I hope.

AGENT   Mum's the word.

WAITER   Absoliwtlee. Now, will this table suit ew?

AGENT   A table's a table, what's important is the company, innit babe? *(To Woman.)*

WAITER   Innit just. Yew are a man after my own 'eart. I can see we're gonna gerron like an 'ighrise on fire. So have a peruse of the menu?

AGENT   What do you recommend?

WAITER   Well, yew couldn't get better than the set meal. Issa paradisal food trek around the Ages of owar Principality…

AGENT   Well, you cook it, I'll eat it.

WAITER   My pleasure. *(To Man)* Take a tip from him, kid. *(To Agent)* Now, wass ewer tipple 'en?

AGENT   What would you suggest?

WAITER   'Ow about a dry Welsh?

AGENT   A dry Welsh!

WAITER   Issa rare wine, so issa bit pricey.

AGENT   The price is irrelevant.

WAITER   Irrelevant?

AGENT   Absolutely.

The Waiter is impressed.

WAITER Yewv got my sortov stomach yew 'ave kid; a gut thass proportional to yewer pocket.

WOMAN Oh God I feel sick. *(To Waiter)* Where's the toilet, dear?

WAITER Issover by there, love.

WOMAN Thank you.

WAITER Yewer in for a treat tonight.

AGENT I can hardly wait.

Exit Waiter.

WOMAN (To Man) Whilst I'm away, whatever he says, don't sign anything.

AGENT Babe, you cut me to the quick.

WOMAN I know you better than you know yourself, Garrie.

Exit Woman

AGENT It's so nice to dine in such charming company.

Pause

AGENT And so we meet at last.

MAN We do?

AGENT I've been waiting for this moment…

MAN   Have you?

AGENT   I've been racking my brains trying to think of who you remind me of. .. But for the life of me, the answer eluded me… then I twigged. It wasn't a 'who' you reminded me of, it was an 'it'.

MAN   A what?

AGENT   An it, a thing, a tick. You remind me of a little African tick.

MAN   Do I?

AGENT   You do, but whereas you stand on street corners like a bubble-wrapped George Fornby, it lies on branches, wrapped in on itself like a rheumatic fist; like a rosebud vampire waiting to draw blood. Sometimes it waits for years… years. The perfect survival machine – waiting; waiting until a lost animal accidentally walks under its branch, then the hungry little bugger drops onto the animal and gorges itself on the victim's blood… How long were you waiting outside my office, Harry?

MAN   Not that long.

AGENT   How did you get my address?

MAN   From a big book full of actresses. At the side of Isabel's photograph was your name. So I found your office, and waited outside for her.

AGENT   For two weeks!

MAN   It was the only way I could think of meeting her.

AGENT   Persistent little bugger, aren't you? At first I thought you were protesting or creating a weird piece of minimalist performance art or something, then I realised that really, you held a black belt in the art of insanity.
'I've got to come and see the loony darling,' Isabel said, 'I've got to come and see him. See you tomorrow at eleven.' So the next day she came.
I was expecting her at ten past, I knew she'd be ten minutes late, she's always ten minutes late; she was ten minutes late for your date tonight wasn't she… I thought she was. I know her you see. I've spent years getting to know her, protecting her, getting frustrated by her, simultaneously loving and hating her; she is my cross and my calvary. Do you understand me? (*Man nods*) I thought you would. So the next morning we sat in my office staring down at you through the window and you stood down there staring up at us from the street. We laughed at you, ridiculed your ridiculousness and destroyed you in the cut of a tongue; all good clean fun, you understand.
Then Bella went strangely quiet and after a while said, 'My God Garrie. My God!' she said, 'He's been waiting for me'. 'Don't be stupid,' I said. 'No, he's waiting to talk to me,' and she was right. You had been waiting for a fortnight on a street corner for a chance to talk to her! What a persistent little bugger Do you mind if I join you ? (*Agent sits next to him.*)

MAN   !

AGENT   Thank you… Let me tell you something Mr Harold Vernon Love-Jones, you don't mind me telling you something do you ?

MAN   No.

AGENT   Not that I'm offering you a choice in the matter. The truth is I don't like you... I don't mean you personally because I don't know you, and it wouldn't matter who you were anyway, it's not you that I don't like, it's what you are, and what you are is normal.
Now you may think that you're Yuri Gagarin, but in the end - you're normal you're boring. You're not like us; not like Bella and me.
Now, I can cope with her affairs with fellow actors which never amount to more than a few casual shags; after all, actors never love actors because they're too much in love with themselves.
But affairs with normal people are dangerous, they could lead to love, marriage, pregnancy and leaving the 'bizz entirely.
I can't allow her to do that, my bank balance couldn't cope with it. So get your plastic paws off her, Harry, because she is my gravy boat and I won't allow you to take her away from me, and I will do everything in my power, everything to make sure that you don't get anywhere near her...
Don't take it personally, I'm only protecting my investment, Harry; it's not the first time that I've squashed a tick. Do I make myself clear?

MAN   Crystal.

Enter Woman.

AGENT   Good, I knew you'd understand...

WOMAN   I thought that you were sitting over there.

AGENT   I was, babe, I was, but Harry looked as lonely as a flapping yunker without you.
His little eyes flashed an SOS across the abyss so I thought I'd better do my Christian duty. I hope you're suitably proud of me. (*Silence*) But I suppose I'd better get going.

WOMAN   Yes, you do that, darling.

AGENT   It was a pleasure talking to you, Harry, I'd love to stay but I know when a carpet's beat. Some other time perhaps . . .perhaps not.

WOMAN   Garrie, please.

AGENT   Patience, babe... it's the mother of all wisdom.

WOMAN   What?

AGENT   Ask a little tick.

WOMAN   What did he say to you?

MAN   Nothing.

WOMAN   Don't beat my bush, darling, just tell me.

MAN   Well... he talked about you...

WOMAN   What about me?

MAN   About you as an actress.

WOMAN   Yes?

MAN   And he said how good you are and how valuable you are to him.

WOMAN   He said that? (*Melts*)

MAN   Yes.

WOMAN   He really thinks that I am a good actress? How good?

MAN   One of the best.

WOMAN   One of the best, darling?

MAN   If not the best.

WOMAN   The best. He really said that?

MAN   My words not his.

WOMAN   He really thinks that I'm the best actress in...?

MAN   ..the world.

WOMAN   The world? Really. He's a dove, isn't he? You're a star Garrie Bright!

AGENT   Your words pierce me, babe.

Waiter enters.

WAITER   Dinner is served, sir.

AGENT   Good, I'm dog hungry.

WAITER   I'm sorry it took so long.

AGENT   Time flies in good company. Doesn't it Harry! So what's my poison then?

WAITER   For starters, a bowl of cawl made from plump Welsh vegetables, stewed to perfection in the juices of Welsh-speaking lambs.

AGENT   Sounds delicious.

WAITER   Issan 'ouse speciality.

AGENT   I can almost taste it... Unfortunately,

WAITER   ... Don't tell me. Yewer a ruddy vegetarian!

AGENT   Is that question or condemnation?

WAITER   Ellsbellsmun! Why didn't 'ew say somethin' earlier?

AGENT   I forgot.

WAITER   Forgot! What do yew mean, bloody 'forgot'. Yew can't forget 'bout food when yewer in a restaurant mun. Is this some kind of new fashion?

AGENT   I had other things on my mind.

WAITER   Just be glad yewer cock's screwed on. So the cawl's out of the question then?

AGENT   Entirely.

WAITER   What if I trawl the meat out with a fork?

AGENT   It won't work.

WAITER Bugger me... I have sweated buckets in tha' kitchen preparin' this meal for yew . It's hell on earth back there, I'll 'ave 'ew know; iss worse than garages in Summer. I've 'alf cooked myself slaving over tha' stove. I'm knackered, now the whole meal's buggered. Why didn't 'ew tell me yew were a veggie earlier?

AGENT I'm sorry.

WAITER Not just for me. Think of the poor lamb whose ruddy life 'as been wasted 'cause of 'ewe'. Pwur dab, he's probably cursin' yew up in sheep's 'eaven and serves 'ew bloody right too. If yewd said at the time I would've cooked 'ew somethin' nutty.

AGENT I said that I'm sorry.

WAITER Sorry don't trim my pork, pal.

AGENT I'm sure we can work this out... (*Hands him a tenner.*)

WAITER Ah, the sweet language of money. Suddenly the kitchen seems a cooler place to be. Back in a tick...

Exit Waiter.

WOMAN God, I hate him. He thinks he can buy everything... including me. Which is ironic because everything he buys, he buys with my money.
He's been leeching my lifeblood for the past twenty years, darling; like a lump fish sucking life from my living. For a vegetarian he's one hell of a vampire; I hate him. But .... I suppose, good agents are as rare as glass houses in Christendom; you can't live with them but you can't live without them..

MAN   You could stop acting.

WOMAN   I've thought about that; thought about it quite a lot actually. But it's easier said than done. What are the prospects for a liar who retires prematurely?

MAN   You could get married.

WOMAN   I'd rather live in Llanelli.

MAN   You could have a child.

WOMAN   I've exhausted that option.

MAN   Don't you want children?

WOMAN   Oh I want children, but children don't want me. I shall live and die alone, darling. My life's like a party when all the interesting people have been and gone; life like the wrinkled words of old friends; my life is a life alone. I wish I could part exchange it like a Honda, but life doesn't work like that, does it?

MAN   That's what makes it interesting.

WOMAN   Well I'm bored with this interesting being and bored with being interested in boring people, darling...

AGENT   So I'm boring, am I, babe?

WOMAN   I wasn't talking to you.

AGENT   To me or about me, your words still kill.

WOMAN   If only they did.

AGENT   It's a fascinating thing, middle age, eh Harry?

WOMAN   You're too alive to be amusing. Shut up, Garrie.

The Waiter enters with food.

WAITER   Open yewer belt and open yewer gob cause 'ere comes the manna, kid.

AGENT   What is this thing?

WAITER   Issa Glamorgan sausage.

AGENT   Is it life size or built to scale?

WAITER   That's as big as they come.

AGENT   Have you read the book *The vegetarian and the art of exploiting him*?

WAITER   No, too rushed off my stumps to read mun, good book izit?

AGENT   This sausage is horizontally challenged.

WAITER   Sh! (*Covers the sausage's ears*) This sausage has gorranart ... don't break it. It may be just a dwt of a thing but as my mam says, 'Morwood. Good things come in small packages; like me, yewer dad and Glamorgan sausages.'

AGENT   Can I eat it?

WAITER   It's an 'undred per cent meat free. And for the main course, I've cooked 'ew my sbeshal concocshun - laverbread curry.

AGENT   I can hardly wait?

WAITER   (*Prepares cork to be popped during speech*) Good, I'm glad tha' yewer 'ungry, cause they're not. Well 'e's 'ungry but e's not eating, and she's not 'ungry, so she's only pickin'. I mean, thass all they 'ad between 'em was a small side salad and a glass of water. I'm a restaurateur norra bloody Weight Watcher! They wouldn' even sniff my Glamorgan sausage! I'm insulted, 'cause iss noh 'alf bad is it?

AGENT   If it was half as big again...

WAITER   Ay, but iss tasty though?

AGENT   Oh yes, it's tasty.

WAITER   Tha's all tha matters 'en ... (*Pops the cork and pours a taster*) Ah! The sweet sound of affluence; brings a tear to my wallet that does. Each time a cork pops a flock of goose pimples land on me... 'Ere, 'ave a sip kid... Wha' do yew reckon en?

AGENT   (*Sips*) It's wet

WAITER   Goes down a treat, don't it. (*Pours a full glass*) From the vines of the Vale thar is; Vale of Glamorgan, see. Complements the sausage geographically. Hey, do yew mind if I um... pull up a pew and ... watch 'ew eat, do yew?

AGENT   Why?

WAITER   It'll be an onar to watch money masticate.

AGENT   Can I object in your restaurant?

WAITER   Thanks mate...

He sits.

WAITER   Tuck in mun, don' stand on ceremony. Pretend I'm not 'ere, don't worry about me... (*Puts feet up*) Ah! Moments of relaxation are like oases in the desert of a god awful day, inney?

AGENT   Are they?

WAITER   Oh ay...Cause, when 'ew boil down to it, life is distilled 'orribleness innit. Iss like a Christmas jigsaw, yew think you gorrit sussed and then 'ew realise that a bit's missin'. Life's like 'a - 'sbloody infuriating. It would be much simpler if we were just like ants, wouldn't it; we didn't 'ave to think, we just scuttle around until some soddin' gardener pink powders us; much easier than 'aving to faff about with all this life business, don't 'ew think so? But it's not goin' to 'appen though is it, cause we're walking brains inwe and God expects every bugger to do their duty... Is that wine really all right?

AGENT   I've tasted worse.

WAITER   Good. 'Cause I 'aven' tasted it myself, see. I took the word of the bloke down the Cash and Carry. Looks all right though, don' it?

AGENT   Would you like some?

WAITER   No, I never drink and serve.

AGENT   Fair enough.

WAITER   But a bit won' 'urt me though, will it?

AGENT   Help yourself.

WAITER   (*Pours himself a glass*)Cheers kid. (*he drinks.*) It's nice to sboil yewerself now an' agen innit ? Cause times are 'ard as Tory 'arts iney ? Ard as Evertons with the middles missing. I'm always on the ruddy go me. My feet 'ave been down so long, when I put them up they get vertigo. Tell 'ew wha though, this is the life mun; the weight off yewer stumps, a bottle of good wine and a sympathetic soul to talk to. Another businessman who understands where yewer comin' from and where yew 'ope to go...

AGENT   I suppose so.

WAITER   So 'ow's life treatin' ew lately 'en?

AGENT   I don't count chickens, but they tend to hatch.

WAITER   Wish I could say the same, but the bottom's dropped out of the pan for me. Wife's bled me dry, kid's turned out to be a bit of a dodo, I know I shouldn't say that, burree 'as though. He sucked all my energy and money then buggered off to oblivion. Then the wife buggered off, cause it turned out she couldn't stand my guts, and I was left on my own; like a blind fish in an art gallery. The last few months 'ave'n' been a bed of oysters, I can tell you... Can I be frank with 'ew, Garrie? Yewer name's Garrie, innit?

AGENT   Ye-es.

WAITER   Thanks, Garrie. See, I am a victim, Gar; a political victim with nowhere to claim asylum, thass wharreyam.

AGENT   Aren't we all?

WAITER   Too true, we're all winnets clinging to a failing democracy, hanging on in there; an 'air's breadth away from catastrophe. But the bummer is, I seem to be more of a victim than most. Not that I'm feeling sorry for myselfs or lookin' for a shoulder to sodden, but over the past few months things 'ave been particularly rough.

AGENT   Times are rough for everyone.

WAITER   Rough as Izal on a baby's bum, mun. So I've been thinkin', perhaps now's the time to move to the right side of the tracks; cause iss the right money that invests in a recession, innit?

AGENT   Move then.

WAITER   Ay, that's what I should do, but thass easier said than done, see. The trouble is, my belt's hitched a bit tight; it's more of a tourniquet than a belt actually. So when I was in the kitchen earlier I thought, 'Morwood, my boy, get yewer thinkin' cap on, it's time to dig yewerself out of this situashun. And as I was cooking yewer meal and half baking my ideas, I kept on thinkin' about wharrew said earlier...

AGENT   What did I say?

WAITER   What did 'ew say? I'll tell 'ew wharrew said. When I said, 'The wine is pricey', yew said 'The price is irrelevant'. Irrelevant, yew said! Without any consideration.

AGENT Did I?

WAITER It was impressive, Gar; it was twenty four carat nonchalance. Yewer obviously a man with nouce and acumen; a Ghetty's Ghetty amongst men. It's why I wanna make 'ew a proposition.

AGENT A proposition!

WAITER Now I know it's a bit off the cuff mun; an unexpected bolt out of the blue, but how does this grab 'ew? I'm prepared to offer yew a blue chip chance to throw yewer lot in with me and invest in my culinary capability.

AGENT You want me to invest in your business?

WAITER That's the long and the short of it, yes...

AGENT Who do you think I am ? Bloody Victor Kayman?

WAITER Gar, I know it's a bit unorthodox, but put it like 'iss, if I was Willy Wonka this would be yewer gold wrapper; dun look a gift 'orse in the mouth wen yewer ridin' 'er. What I'm offerin yew is the chance of a lifetime, mun; a dibenture in vegetarian 'eaven. Invest in my restaurant Gar, and we'll rake in the dosh, and yew'll never again have to pay through the nose for a meatless meal. So what do you think then? Is it a deal?

AGENT Oh, for God's sake! (*Drawn towards Man and Woman*)

WAITER   Just mull it over, don't sieve me out.

AGENT   I've got an emergency to think about!

WAITER   I squeezed yew in tonight, yew should squeeze me!

AGENT   All right, but I can't promise you anything! I'll see what I can do. In the mean time I have more pressing matters...

Cut to Man and Woman.

WOMAN   ...Darling, I've suffered more fools than you've had hot dinners. It's the occupational hazard of womanhood; biting the bullshit and swallowing.

MAN   Am I a fool?

WOMAN   Undoubtedly, darling. Most men are. They are the appendix of a woman's lot; they're in there for some reason but you're not sure why, so when they play up you might as well get rid of them.

MAN   Do you hate me because I'm a man then?

WOMAN   Don't be paranoid, darling, you have gripped my heart with a sincerity that's as scarce as a lone bus. From the moment we met I felt a comfortableness between us; like lying in a womb of down when the lightning's forking.

MAN   That's nice.

WOMAN   Just words, words poached from some turgid play I died ten deaths in. The second time you stopped me, I felt a knowing; to know is an odd sort of feeling; an irrational thumb to suck. I don't know why I came on this date with you. I just knew that I had to. I had to see you. I surprised myself with my own certainty. I'm not an impulsive sort of woman. Ordinarily I don't mix'n'match with any Tom Dick and Harry. There's the world, and then there's me. That way it's less trouble....

MAN Cleaner...

WOMAN Easier... but the day I met you... the day I met you, Harry, I wanted to dirty my hands...

AGENT Wash out that spot, babe!

WOMAN Bugger off and die!

AGENT You splay my heart.

WOMAN If only, Garrie, if only...

Focus on Agent and Man.

WAITER She don' like 'ew very much, does she?

AGENT (*As quote*) 'Her syllables scythe me to the quick; her words flay me to the core; her sentences shatter my bones; when she sings - I die.'

WAITER Exactly, she 'ates 'ew.

AGENT Why does she cripple me whilst crutching him - the Woolworths Yuri Gagarin?

WAITER   Why do women do anythin, I ask 'ew? One day it's a new bathroom suite, the next day they're divorcin' 'ew. They're all soddin' unfathomable, deep as cysts, mun; she's just the same dap as the rest of 'em.

AGENT   No. Don't blame her, it's him. He's the little tick. She's just an actress crying out for love and protection - that's why she pays her fifteen percent... Do you have somewhere quiet where we can chat?

WAITER   In the kitchen.

AGENT   Good. It seems that I might be in a position to raise your Titanic after all.

WAITER   Yewll scratch my back 'en?

AGENT   If you'll reciprocate.

WAITER   What do yew want me to do?

AGENT   Take a tick then squash it.

They exit. Man and Woman left alone.

WOMAN   It must be daybreak. The leech has squirmed back into his coffin.

MAN   It's only about half eight.

WOMAN   Wishful thinking, darling, wishful thinking. God, I hate that man...

MAN   Why don't you leave him?

WOMAN   I'm legally bound to the prat. I think the only way I'll get rid of Garrie will be to drive a stake through our contract.
He's a Poxy little creature, isn't he? He treats me like his property. Well, I'm fed up of feeling as if I'm beholden to him; as if we're married or he's my Siamese twin or something. Oh yes, he served his purpose at one stage but he never cared about my career, he never steered me towards the prestigious jobs that led onto somewhere.
My talent has been wasted... wasted, darling! It makes me livid to think about it. When you've felt all your life as if you're destined for the stars, and in the end the only stars you see are reflections in the gutter; when you're directed by kids half your age, who earn twice your wage, it's hard not to be bitter. I'm as bitter as batteries on the tongue. Do you know that taste, darling?

MAN   No. I've never had ambition.

WOMAN   You must be a happy man.

MAN   I have too much fear within me.

WOMAN   God, we're a pair of sad sods, aren't we. The Fear and Bitterness of Bella and Bubble Man; sounds like a book by Hunter S. Thompson...

MAN   I haven't read it.

WOMAN   I wouldn't bother, darling, you'd die of fright by chapter three. That's what puzzles me, Harry, if you're so afraid of everything why don't you fear my rejection? Why do you trust me when I could spit you

out like dead chewing gum?
I lied to you once, I could lie again. I could lie you senseless; lie 'till you reeled like cherries on a bandit; reject you like a bad film on eject.

MAN But you won't.

WOMAN Why won't I?

MAN Because of regret.

WOMAN Is that a fact? (*Half pause*) Damn your sincerity! Why are you so bloody sincere, Harry?

MAN I can't be anything else.

WOMAN Can't you? So ... what did my agent say to you, eh? ... Hand on heart, Harry! Did he really call me the best actress in the world?.. Did he? No more lies... Did he eulogize me?

MAN No.

WOMAN I thought not! The little git!

MAN I'm sorry.

WOMAN It's too late. You're a man, I knew you couldn't be that perfect. And by the way, what's your standard of beauty? Was it just a beautiful lie to call me beautiful?

MAN I meant every syllable of it.

WOMAN Bullshit, I've found you out once. How can I believe you again? You have lied to me. You had the gall to demand honesty when you yourself had lied.

MAN I lied not to hurt you.

WOMAN Typical male hypocrisy.

MAN I won't lie again.

WOMAN Your chips are wet darling.

MAN I'm really sorry...

WOMAN And I thought we had something....Well, more fool me! So, having destroyed the truth and gutted the lie, what are we left with, eh?

MAN Honesty?

WOMAN Honesty! That's a can of scorpions if ever there was one. Honesty's a painful admission. It never precedes the event; it only precedes a plea for clemency. There's bugger all honest about honesty, darling!

He begins to take off his helmet.

WOMAN What are you doing?

MAN I want to be completely honest with you!

WOMAN I'm not sure whether I want such honesty.

MAN But we must grow in trust.

WOMAN I loathe responsibility.

MAN Why?

WOMAN I can't stomach guilt of any description!

MAN Don't be guilty, this is my decision.

WOMAN But is it the right one?

MAN It's not the wrong one.

WOMAN Just keep your bubble on, Harry! If you took it off now the shock might kill you, then I'd be dead bloody guilty. I'd feel as if I was your mother and I don't want to be any bugger's mother, darling!

MAN I don't want another mother!

WOMAN Good! I'm glad! I don't want to kissed by the lips of any complex kisser!

His helmet is off. We hear his natural voice for the first time.

MAN My mother's dead!

WOMAN Thank God for that! (*Pause of realisation.*) Oh God. I'm truly sorry...

MAN Don't apologise.

WOMAN I'm dreadfully dreadfully sorry, darling...

MAN ...Don't be. I wasn't sorry.

WOMAN Weren't you?

MAN   No, there was no reason to be, my mother blazed in glory. She died clutching my father. They were inseparable in death as in life, like chicken breasts clumped in a freezer.

WOMAN   (*After a pause*) How did they die?

MAN   In a car crash. The flames seared their flesh until there remained only two ash statues grinning through their teeth.

WOMAN   Horrific.

MAN   Almost exotic? (*With irony*) After their memorial service I gutted their house and coated it entirely in plastic.

WOMAN   Plastic?

MAN   Yes. It's not prone to rot like flesh and love, it's clinically comfy and easily disinfected. And when I'd covered everything, I closed the front door and sealed myself within.
Plastic time passed in clouds of thought; as if my life was on auto playback re-screening each feeling and perception... and one image kept recurring again and again.
It was 1969 and I was moonwalking along Valhalla Avenue wearing the plastic space suit which I'd just been given for my eighth birthday. It was raining, the first time I'd ever been out on my own in the wet, but I was secure, safe from the rain in my NASA helmet. I was ecstatic - glide walking on all planets simultaneously. I was irridescent - like the colour of sound in a Gorecki symphony. I was happy beyond

heaven, until my mother screamed me back to earth with a - 'Gerrowt of the wet, you'll catch your death, you stupid bugger' - She clipped my wings, and for that reason I always hated her. But now that she's dead...

WOMAN ...You could almost forgive her? (*Ironic*)

MAN No. I realise that there's nothing to forgive. It took me nine months to realise that; nine months of plastic isolation to realise that I didn't want to... (*He can hardly say it*) shag her and I didn't want to kill her, I wanted to thank her.

WOMAN Thank God for that.

MAN And upon realising that, nine months to the day of my cocoonment, I felt an overpowering urge; the sort of urge that makes you want to scratch a teacup because it cannot scratch its own itch. I felt compelled to unwrap the television, plug it in and turn it on, which is not like me, ordinarily I loathe the thing. But I turned it on, sat in front of it and waited. First there was darkness; the last instant of being alone. Then there was a voice; your voice followed by colour. Then both your body and voice were one, advertising bath cleaner.

WOMAN God, how embarrassing!

MAN No, you were beautiful.

WOMAN How beautiful, darling?

MAN The most beautiful woman in the world.

WOMAN   Is that a probably?

MAN   That's an absolutely.

WOMAN   Really?

MAN   No more lies, Isabel.

Pause.

WOMAN   Harry, I can't promise you anything.

MAN   Then promise nothing, it'll save you lying.

WOMAN   Dance with me, darling.

They dance. The Agent and the Waiter are in the kitchen area behind glass.

AGENT   The chips are down, the price is good, so will you do it, Morwood?

WAITER Thass the sixty four thousand dollar Gar, bu' murder's not a chip shop decishun; iss 'ardly a 'shall I ave the fish or the chicken' mun? To be 'onest, I'm in two minds; I'm like a brain sliding down a blade... Will I or won' I? Either way I'll be buggered by regret, especially if I don't do it. And if I do do it, 'ow would I snuff 'im? I mean, I couldn't cope with the 'ands on approach. It would be a bit too embarrassing; I wouldn't know where to look mun, and wa' the 'ell would I say to 'im as I kill im? 'Sorry bout this, but, but the weather's pickin' up a treat innit'? No, I'd feel as embarrassed as God in a chapel kid.

AGENT   Then what about poison? Poison's less intimate.

WAITER Poison is. Trouble is, he don eat an' drink!

AGENT   Then make 'im.

WAITER 'Ow?

AGENT   Think, Morwood, think...

WAITER (*After a thought*) Wha' do yew think I'm doin! I've go' more thought in me than a mensa brain. I am thinking! Thass half my problem, see, Gar, cause wa' I'm thinkin' is this, if I cobble a plan together an irrall goes slick as a quiff, there's still a liggl niggle, see.

AGENT   Spit it out.

WAITER Well, how in 'ell's name do we get rid of the body?

AGENT   I've been thinking about that.

WAITER 'Issa knicker twister, innit.

AGENT   And you said you were thinking, Morwood. Think again. This isn't a meat free restaurant, is it?

WAITER Course not.

AGENT   Well then, long pig's á la mode in the smoke apparently.

WAITER Wha!

AGENT   Under the arm is a bit of OK, and the bum is pretty tasty.

WAITER   Tharriss disgusting!

AGENT   I prefer to use the term 'cannibalistically enterprising' - diversification is, after all, the key to economic recovery, don't you agree, Morwood?

WAITER   For twenty-five grand I'd be inclined to agree with anything, but the thought of eatin' Arry makes me a bit squitty, Gar.

AGENT   Just think of the money, Morwood, think of the money...

WAITER   Don' worry, I am. Iss my only thought, kid. But money don' buy courage, does it? Look, when the clogs pop, I'm the back 'arf of a coward, Gar; when death hits the fan I run the mile faster than Bannista'.

AGENT   Well I'm hardly a veteran in the field.

WAITER   Ay, but death seems to come natural to yew.

AGENT   I feed off my fear, that's what you should do. Just feed off your fear and picture a restaurant, Morwood... a little restaurant on the right side of the tracks. That little restaurant could be your little restaurant... you could own that little restaurant if you get rid of one little man; one little man stands between you and your dream. Snuff one little man and your dream could be realised; your fantasy could be your life... our lives. For that one man's death is worth two men's dreams... two men's lives; your life... and mine. So his existence is in essence a selfish act, to kill him is a blessing, Morwood... A blessing... It's either you or him. Stew here in gastronomic obscurity or serve the palates that will appreciate your culinary capability, You want to move to the right side of the tracks don't you, Morwood?

WAITER   Of course I do.

AGENT   Then it's up to you....

WAITER   I wannw get out of this 'ole, I've gorrw.

AGENT   Of course you have to.

WAITER   My talent has being ignored.

AGENT   Wasted.

WAITER   Wasted! I'm a root-bound cactus in need of repotting.

AGENT   ...You're vegetating .

WAITER   Stagnatin'. Goin nowhere, over-gifted and under-rated... Bugger it! Less trash 'im kid.

AGENT   Morwood, that is the ticket. So, unfurl your plan and let's get on with it .

Man and Woman are dancing.

AGENT   How touching.

WOMAN   For God's sake! You're as unfeeling as a leper's hand!

AGENT   Sorry, babe, I don't know what came over me.

WOMAN   You came over yourself again, Garrie. *(To Man)* Let's leave, darling.

AGENT   You can't leave yet.

WOMAN   Just watch us go.

AGENT   They can't leave yet, can they, Morwood?

WAITER No, no... Issowt of the queschun.

WOMAN   Just bring me the bill.

WAITER Bugger the bill, mun! This is a do or die situashun.

WOMAN   Is it?

WAITER Damn right irris. God knows where my 'ead was when yew came in earlier. Middle of next week probably. I've got so much floatin' 'round my mind, my brain's like a bloody estuary. Yew can't leave yet.

WOMAN   Why?

WAITER Cause... of the *(he fishes for a reason)*... tradition, kid.

WOMAN   Tradition?

WAITER Oh ay, *(improvising)* I was only reminded of it when I was frying the fat with Gar in the kitchen. 'You know it's their first date, don't you?' he said. 'First date!' I said. 'Yes' he said. 'Oh God' I said - cause I'd clean forgotten about the tradition, see, and we can't afford to turn a blind eye to tradition, can we? Iss like a pit bull barring owar path, we can't ignore it. It defines where we are, where we've come from and more importantly where we don't wannw go, and if we don't respect it we're ruddy done for. Well I wouldn't 'ave been done for, but yew two would've been dog food.

MAN   What do you mean ?

WAITER   Pin back yewer lug oles an' clock 'is kid. All the couples tharr 'ave spent their first dates 'ere 'are still appy as Larry; all the couples tharriss apart from two. They both died in horrific car crashes not long after eatin' 'ere.

WOMAN   Are you sure their deaths were car related ?

WAITER   My kitchens are daily disinfected, I'll 'ave 'ew know

MAN   So their deaths are a mystery then?

WAITER   Not to me. I know the real reason why they copped it. They died 'cause of the 'tradition', see, kid, and 'cause the tradition wasn' respected.

MAN   What tradition?

WAITER   Yew may well ask... There's a tradition in this restaurant that we toast first dates for good luck. Unfortunately, I didn't toast the two couples that died- it slipped my mind completely. And to think that I was goin' to let yew walk out of this restaurant without toasting yew. The consequences could've been dire; yew were a sip's breath away from disaster... a sip's breath kid.

MAN   Thank God you remembered.

WAITER   *(Points)* He probably prompted me; cause I'm a dull bugger, see. Acting twp iss my only talent, I've gorra great aptitude for it; Still. A sip in time is better late than never, mun? So, before you ge' goin', less make sure yew don't pop yewer clogs by poppin a bottle open. *(He produces a bottle of champagne and four glasses)* 'W fancies a little toast 'en?

WOMAN   Not for me.

WAITER   Ellsbells, are yew shwer mun?

WOMAN   Perfectly.

AGENT   It's for your own good.

WOMAN   Drink bleach, Garrie!

(Both couples split into asides.)

AGENT   *(To Woman)* To the bone, baby, to the bone. *(To Man)* What about you, Harry?

MAN   Whatever Isabel wants is fine by me. *(Man is worried though.)*

AGENT   I admire a man who's got the nerve to knock knock God... You've got guts, boy, I admire that. I admire it! What a pity to see such courage wasted. Such a pity.

WAITER   A ruddy shame...

AGENT   Still, if you must dare the tradition... Rest in peace, Harry. *(Aside)* Well re-invented, Morwood?

WAITER   All's fear in love and war kid.

Focus on Man and Woman

MAN Please, Isabel. Tonight is our only first date. We'll never have another one. What if the waiter is right? We can't afford to dare the tradition? I don't want you to die and I don't want us to die, not when 'our' life is just beginning. To me the slightest risk is not a risk worth taking. Don't you think so?

WOMAN .. I don't know... How can I know... How can you know...How can we know? That's all I know is, I loathe ceremonies, darling.

MAN What are a few words and a sip of Champagne, Isabel?

WOMAN Suffocating.

MAN But we can t afford to ignore the tradition.

WOMAN Why?

MAN Because 'I'... 'I've' been dead too long to want to die!

WOMAN Ah! First it was an 'us', now it's an 'I'. Isn't our new found honesty an amazing thing, Harry? Well, as you seem to be more honest with me, I'll be more honest with you. If I agree to act my part, I want you to understand one thing, it doesn't mean that I've hitched my horse to your wagon. I can carve my own trail. Do you understand that, darling?

MAN Of course.

WOMAN That's not to say that I won't love you. But one ceremony does not make an eternity. Do you understand me, Harry?

MAN   Sure. If that's how you feel.

WOMAN   That's how I feel and you must respect my feelings and accept them without question.

MAN   Without question?

WOMAN   That's how it has to be.

MAN   So I have no choice in the matter?

WOMAN   Not if you love me. You see, throughout my life I've been a passenger, darling. I've allowed myself to be driven down roads that I wouldn't particularly choose to drive down.
It's taken me this long to realise that I don't need to hail a taxi, I can drive myself where I want, when I want and at a pace that suits me, I want to travel with you, Harry. But if we travel together, we must travel as equals or else we travel alone, darling.

MAN   I want to journey whenever, wherever whatever

AGENT   Time for a blessing, Morwood. Think of a little restaurant and do what you have to do, pop that cork and let a flock of goose pimples land on you...

The Agent goes over to the Man and Woman. Waiter pops the cork and sometime during the next speech, he poisons one glass.

AGENT   Champagne, cocaine, Mozart and men! - abused either on their own or in any combination; that is the hedonistic fourfold path to heaven. Men, I can give or take, cocaine I've given up and though I adore Mozart to death, it has to be the Champagne for me. I find it so sartorially fulfilling. I always reach enlightenment before dropping out of this world in a blaze of glory. What about you, Harry? Do you want to blaze or splutter like a damp squib; an embarrassment to both host and party?

MAN   I think I'd rather blaze after a long fuse.

AGENT   Good, very good *(He is handed a glass)* Thank you, Morwood. Is this Harry's glass?

WAITER   Irris, iss poured with a special blessing.

AGENT   Lucky Harry, a special blessing. Blaze on this boy, the only bubble worth desiring... And what about you, babe? Are you going to raise a flame or raze a forest as you normally do?

WOMAN   Rise or raze, at least I've risen. You couldn't rise above or raise anything, could you?

AGENT   What is that supposed to mean?

WOMAN   Nothing, darling...Just a small glass for me.

AGENT   It'll be my pleasure.

WOMAN   Only yours, Garrie.

AGENT   Scarcd to the flesh. *(She is handed a glass)*

WOMAN   Why don't you burn in hell...

AGENT   I am already there, baby.

WAITER   *(Aside)* She'll gut yewer garters, kid.

AGENT   Just propose the toast, Morwood. *(He takes a glass)*

WAITER   *(Declaims)* May I propose a toast?

AGENT   Of course you can, just get on with it!

WAITER   Well pardon me for pwppin'.

AGENT   Shut up and start toasting!

WAITER   Wharrever yew say kid... On behalf of all the staff of Welsh Rarebits... Well iss only me at the moment but I 'ope to expand in the near future; move to the right side of the tracks where the discerning palates are. 'Cause it's the wise money that invests in a depression, innit, Gar?

AGENT   Wise money, Morwood.

WAITER   Damn right, kid. Diversification and expansion are the roads to economic recovery. Don' 'ew agree, Gar?

AGENT   Absolutely.

WAITER   But I won t bore yew with my ambition, cause I'm sure you've go' skyscrapin' 'opes of yewer own; tracks yew wanna cross and roads yew wanna drive down. So without further ado, let me propose a real Welsh Rarebits toast. To Isabel an 'Arry.

AGENT   I'll drink to that!

WOMAN   Darling, I've got more than you

Woman swaps glasses with man and downs her glass in one, this is seen by the agent and the waiter.

AGENT   Babe!

WAITER Ellsbellsmun!

AGENT   Oh my God!

WOMAN   What's wrong, darling?

AGENT   Nothin'

WAITER Thass cooked owar goose tharrave, kid.

AGENT   Bloody Hell, Morwood... Did my eyes lie, or did I see, what I saw?

WAITER Believe me, yew saurit

AGENT   Shit. Send for a doctor.

WAITER Don't be stupid, I've gorrw think of my business, mun.

AGENT   Bugger your business, she might die.

WAITER She's worm food, kid; 'might' don' even enter into the equashun.

AGENT   Oh my God, Morwood...

WOMAN   ...What are you two prattling on about?

AGENT   The transience of life, babe, the brevity of beauty. *(To*

Waiter) She is my manna from heaven, her words feed me. Without her I am nothing. What am I going to do?

WAITER I don' know abowt yew, but I'm gonna get 'er ' coat, kid.

AGENT What for?

WAITER It'll give 'er the impression that everythin's all right and she's about to go.

AGENT Of course she's about to go, quicker than she expects to!

WAITER Ay, but we don' wannw panic 'er unnecessarily. If we act as if nothing's wrong she might pop off quietly.

AGENT You amaze me, Morwood; from Schweitzer to Crippen at the drop of a hat.

WAITER Juss feed off yewer fear, kid, thass wa' yew said to me.

AGENT That was when I was talking about him. Isabel's a different story. How long does she have left?

WAITER I'm not sure.

AGENT Give me the poison... How much did you give her?

WAITER I'm an instinctive chef, I just woppt irrin.

AGENT That explains your cooking.

Waiter exits to get her coat.

WOMAN   What's hitting the fan, darling?

AGENT   Nothing.

WOMAN   You're greaseproof, Garrie. I have a nose when you're lying.

AGENT   Exception to the rule, babe.

WOMAN   Don't treat me like a pert arse. I don't feel very well and I'm running out of patience.

MAN   Perhaps we should go.

WOMAN   Not yet, Harry. Spill your beans, Garrie.

AGENT   There's nothing to spill.

WOMAN   You're brimming with guilt, just tell me!

AGENT   What can I say?

WOMAN   The truth, darling. There's something wrong and I want to know what it is.

AGENT   Well... I suppose you've got a perfect right to know.

WOMAN   Know what?

AGENT   There's been a bit of conflag, babe. It's all Morwood's fault. I tried to dowse his anger in the kitchen but he was so incensed, I just couldn't stop him seeking it.

WOMAN   Seeking what?

AGENT   Revenge; sweet, simple revenge. Retaliation by poison.

WOMAN   Who's been poisoned?

AGENT   Well... To put your mind at rest, babe, you'll be pleased to know that it's not me

WOMAN   That's hardly a consolation.

AGENT   But because the person in question wouldn't even nibble Morwood's Glamorgan Sausage, the object of his rage was Harry.

MAN   I'm fine.

AGENT   As he should be. You see, unfortunately, babe... unfortunately for you that is... by swapping glasses with Harry you accidentally drank the poisoned Champagne that was meant for him.

WOMAN   Are you pulling both legs, darling?

AGENT   No. Serious to the nth degree. You are playing at home to poison, baby. It's all Morwood's fault, all his doing... I tried my best to stop him...

Waiter enters.

WAITER Thass codswallop kid!

AGENT   Don't deny it, Morwood.

WAITER Yewer lyin' mun.

AGENT   Own up to it like a man.

WAITER   I own up to nothing. Yew asked me to murder 'im

AGENT   So you admit to it then.

WAITER   It was yew w' gave 'im the glass!

AGENT   After you'd put the poison in.

WAITER   See, now he admits it too. The bugger's up to 'is neck in it.

AGENT   All right! So I did what I did! But what I did, I did it for you, baby!

WOMAN   For me... For me! You're always doing bloody things for me things; that I've never wanted you to do in the first place Garrie!

AGENT   Sorry, babe. I just couldn't sit back and watch you being whisked away by a Woolies Yuri Gagarin. You are my babe and I am your darling. You belong to me, I belong to you. We are meant for each other, I have the contract to prove it.

WOMAN   What good's your contract when I'm dead. Love cannot be appropriated, Garrie Bright.

AGENT   *(After a thought)* You're right, damn right. But we have a contract, we are eternally tied, we shall never be parted. I'm coming after you. You can't desert me.. I'll be your agent until death and beyond. *(He poisons his own glass)*

WOMAN   For God's sake stop him!

AGENT   I demand my fifteen percent of everything - including eternity. *(He raises his glass.)*

WOMAN   Fuck off Garrie!

The Agent drinks. Silence.

MAN   *Sorry.*

WOMAN   Don't be.

MAN   But it's all my fault..

WOMAN   For God's sake leave me my dignity Harry *(She laughs. She begins to fade.)*

MAN   What's funny?

WOMAN   Déja vu on the edge of death.

MAN   You've been here before?

WOMAN   Yes.

MAN   You've been in this restaurant? *(Almost accusingly)*

WOMAN   No. In this situation.

MAN   Oh... When?

WOMAN   When the coal tip used to eclipse the horizon, darling. When I used to go round in a gang with three boys; two ugly, one beguiling. *(She finds it more and more difficult to speak)* One Winter, in an empty house, where an old woman had once died behind the door, we used to play a game of cards. A sort of trumps, where the boy with the winning hand would get to neck me after a fashion. I was the stake; I was passion won or lost on the turn of a card. The uglies won their hands alternately; first one ugly, then the other; the beguiling one was always the loser; Once won, an ugly would suck me to his lips, whilst the other counted hippopotamuses; One hippopotamus, two hippopotamus ...the count became slower from week to week, night to night, kiss to kiss; each caress watched by the beguiling one who never missed a trick, but lost every hand. One night I said, 'let me kiss the little one just for the hell of it.' 'But he's never kissed before' they said 'He wouldn't know how to do it' 'I've watched enough!' said the little one, and for his cheek, ten hippopotamuses were granted...

She draws Harry to her lips.

WOMAN I guided his mouth to mine and gave him the sweetest of kisses to the accompaniment of ten hippopotamuses. And when we'd been counted out, breathless on the canvas, we kept on kissing... I am still kissing him now, darling.

They kiss.

WOMAN My words are my armour Harry... but now, words fail me.

She dies in a kiss.

AGENT I won't be long, babe... I'll get you good contracts up there, I'll work harder on your behalf than I ever did down here. I'll get you work that will lead on to somewhere, God knows where, but it'll be somewhere. *(He begins to fade)* You'll be the toast of Heaven, babe. I promise...

WAITER   Oi. Bright spark! Before yew fizzle out, I 'ope yewer not gonna forget owar deal?

AGENT   What deal?

WAITER   Don' play silly buggers, Gar. Now coff up the twenty-five grand tha' yew promised me kid.

AGENT   Mission not accomplished .

WAITER   It wasn't my fault there was a cock-up, yew were in charge of the handlin' department, yew can't blame me.

AGENT   I can blame whoever I want, I'm a dying man, so stuff this in your life cover and smoke it. I never had any intention of investing in your restaurant, I'd rather have paid to have had my nails extracted; one by one...painfully. Do you understand me?

WAITER   I can't believe what yewar sayin'.

AGENT   Well open your ears and listen good. Your restaurant is loathsome, your food is putrid and you are revolting, Morwood.

WAITER   Yew can't mean that, mun.

AGENT   It's probably the only thing that I've ever meant in my whole life; an honour reserved solely for you. And for you, Harry, I hope we never cross paths again from here to eternity. Good riddance and goodbye...Don't sign anything till I arrive, baby!

The Agent dies.

WAITER   Well thass put the kaybosh on tha' then... S'just yew and me agen, kid. *(Embarrassment)* Fancy some laverbread curry to take yewer mind off everythin'? Plenty left in the pot if yew want some.

MAN   No thank you.

WAITER   Can't say I blame 'ew, iss bloody revoltin' mun. *(pauses)* God!

MAN   Have you ever loved, Morwood?

WAITER   Wha'? People you mean?

MAN   A person.

WAITER   I dunnow, kid.

MAN   I think I did.

WAITER   Lucky yew 'en. I just went through the mowshuns, me, and I didn't even do tha' very successfully. I barely stayed the course, kid; a waste all round when I think about it. When the boy flew the coop, me and the wife went on an 'oliday to Ireland, thought it'd be romantic like, but i' wasn't...
On owar own for the first time ever, we argued black 'n blue; worse soddin' 'oliday I ever 'ad; painful as piles, apart from one day when we wen' on a trip over to this island. Three hours of multicoloured 'ell to

reach an invisible jewel; a grey rock set in a grey ring of sky and sea.
The missus 'ated it, burreye loved it me, cause i' was... honest, I know i' sounds stupid, burri' was. The island was 'honest', I can't think of any other word forrit, cause there was no earth to 'ide the bones of the planet... just shameless stone. The most naked place I'd ever been in, there was no escapin' anythin'. It was like walkin' the ribs of a famine victim. By dinner we'd walked to the foot of an 'ill which 'ad a fort on top of it. Well, the wife thought enough's enough an' stayed in the café, but I wanted to go on. It was my Everest and I 'ad to conquer it... and I did.
The fort turned out to be an 'uge 'orse shoe of a stone perched on a cliff three 'undred feet above the sea, three 'undred feet they said but it seemed more like three 'undred miles to me. 'Cause the fort seemed to be suspended in the sky at that peak of its movement. You know, like tha' moment when an engine cuts out and a plane 'angs there before fallin', or a ball stops dead before droppin'.
I walked right up to the edge of the cliff kid, no fences stopping me, and I stood on the knife edge of the Atlantic. Behind me was the 'ole of Europe, in front of me next stop America, behind me the past, in front of me the future, and I was there; the most alive I could ever be and I wanted to leap off and fly like I used to leap off the rocks and soar over Ogmore beach when I was an immortal kid.
'Cause on that cliff edge there was no Morwood. There was no fort, there was no wife an' no God, it was as if the whole universe was flowing through me. I was like the neck of an egg-timer that turns eternally. And on the blade's edge, the 'appiest moment I'd ever 'ad in my life, I suddenly thought about the wife, and I

thought, 'I bet yew she's feeling the same thing in the caffee.' An' I reckon she was, cause when we got back, the first thing she did was divorce me. I envy yew, kid, to think yew have loved is better than knowing for a dead cert tha' yew haven't.
(He goes to the Man - he has died of fear) Are you alright, kid?... Kid! Don't play silly sods wi' me. Wha' are yew trying to do - bugger my business completely? Ay, tha means all of 'ew, mun...

He starts to uncork a bottle of wine.

WAITER   Don't speak to me 'en... See if I care... Long pig's á la mode in the smoke so they say... under the arms a birrov OK and the bum is pretty tasty... What was 'a? O ay, for plastic I'd rip open yewer kidney and cook i' just as you like i', diversification is after all the key to economic recovery. Don' 'ew agree?

He uncorks the bottle.

WAITER   Ah, the sweet language of money. I can feel a flock of goose pimples land on me.

Lights fade to black as he drinks.

Hawlfraint/Copyright IAN ROWLANDS MAY '95

LOVE IN PLASTIC

Love in Plastic. Chris Morgan and Kath Dimmery

Photo Dave Roxburgh

NOTES ON THE PLAY

WOMAN: Words mean nothing, they are the currency of men. I should bloody know, I've surrounded myself long enough in them. My words are irrelevant, the battle is the unravelling. Not that I hold out much hope of being understood or of understanding anyone.

MAN: Why?

WOMAN: I've been an actress too long to believe in communication.

It has been written that humans can never truly communicate; with regard to touch - there will always be a layer of moisture between two skins, with regard to thought - as it is subject to a process of mutation, the probability of communication pure thought is slight.

Our only hope is love, for though it might not offer the possibility of communication, it offers us the chance to suspend our disbelief that we are, if only for an instant, not alone.

Ian Rowlands

"Our brain, our very bodies have become this bubble, this sanitised sphere, a transparent envelope in which we seek refuge, as destitute and unprotected as the unborn child condemned to artificial immunity and perpetual transfusions, condemned to die as soon as he will have kissed his mother. To each his own bubble, that is the law today.' Jean Baudrilard *The Ecstasy of Communication*.

LOVE IN PLASTIC

'Seeing comes before words. The child looks and recognises before it can speak'
John Berger - *Ways of Seeing*

Although the word is central to the work of Theatr y Byd, the company is also keen to use the visual image to carry the message of the drama to the audience. Since 1992, the company has explored a multi-media approach to its work as part of its artistic policy and has on numerous occasions commissioned artists to work with it.

Sometimes the commissioned works have been created as a reaction to the work as in *The Sin Eaters* (1992) and *Solomon's Glory* (1993), where artists worked either in rehearsal or just with the spoken word and the resulting artworks were displayed in a space near the performance. In the later productions of *Glissando on an Empty Harp* (1994) and *Love in Plastic* (1995), the resulting artwork became an integral element in the production.

The artist Tim Davies was commissioned to create an installation for the production of *Love in Plastic* which opened at the Glynn Vivian Art Gallery in Swansea on May 25th 1995.

It was created in close collaboration with the company and it was shown at the gallery for a month prior to the premiére of the play as an artwork itself.

Tim Davies took the image of the plucked rose as a symbol of the entanglement in the play as he explains

"The rose. A plucked rose. For centuries a message of love and dreams was seen captured in its dying glory between sheets of perspex. Compressed and suspended for eternity. The flower gradually decaying between the force of this undying material.

Any train journey will witness the strewn débris on convenient banks, undying and permanent amounts the seasonal growth.

And here lies Harold. His hopes, his dreams, eternal but ultimately suffocated by his own fears and seclusions within his exposed internalized world."

The installation, which Davies called Caress, was used in the production as a wall of perspex panels of dying roses suspended between the kitchen and the restaurant as a constant echo of the mood of the play. Sheets of black plastic were also used in the background to represent more solid walls.

Plastic is at the forefront of Harold's life. For nine months since his parents' death in a car crash, he has lived in their house which he has gutted and encased in plastic.

Harold: "It's not prone to rot like flesh and love, it's clinically comfy and easily disinfected. And when I'd covered everything, I closed the front door and sealed myself within."

From within his protected plastic house he struggles with his resentment towards his mother. The recurrent memory of the delight he experienced when he wore the plastic spacesuit he had been given for his eighth birthday helps him break out of his melancholy. He unwraps the plastic sheet off the television, plugs it in, and falls in love with the actress he sees in a bath cleaner advertisement.

As he ventures into the outside world to find the actress, he takes his plastic protection with him by wearing a space suit.

Written in South Walian English, the play skims the outer surface of the characters with humorous clichés while touching the fears and insecurities hiding beneath. The waiter in the restaurant hides behind his 'pre-recorded crowd atmos' played to give the impression the place is full and he is successful; the actress lies 'to survive' while her agent fears losing her to Harold. In all his plays, Ian Rowlands manages through careful manipulation of language and plot, to create a text with many layers of meaning. By using specially composed music by Robin Williamson and Lawson Dando and the installation by Tim Davies in *Love in Plastic*, he has been able to add even more strands and layers which offer more than one way into the play's meaning.

Jill Piercy   Spring 1999

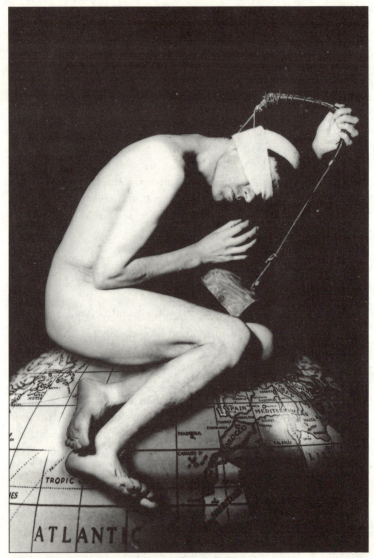

Glissando on an Empty Harp (after G.F.Watts) photo Dave Heke

Glissando on an Empty Harp

Glissando on an Empty Harp was first performed at the Taliesin Arts Centre, Swansea on the 3rd of March 1994.

Cast

HEAD/FERGUS - **Dafydd Wyn Roberts**
WOMAN - **Julie Gibbs**
EMRYS - **Philip Michell**
ERIC - **Ian Rowlands**

∞

director - **Ian Rowlands**
technical manager/lighting Designer - **Dave Roxburgh**
designer - **Penni Bestic**
stage manager - **David Thompson/Alex Lemmon**
costume design - **Siân Elin Jenkins**
original music - **Lawson Dando/ Matthew Rowlands**

The 'head' character was entirely video projected during the performance. The video elements were filmed in a specially commissioned installation designed by Martina Galvin. The video production was by Terry Dimmick and Dave Heke.

Open on a dark stage. A video plays. The character on the video is 'the Head': the speaking Fergus.

HEAD Between you, me and these four walls, I don't like it very much in here. The company's not too hot, if you know what I mean. Like exhibition openings at shoe box galleries where the odour of sweat, white wine, oil and bad breath condenses in sickly sweet pockets of pretension; like being in cafés where men call you cabs, call you sir then spit in your coffee; like being a vegetarian in a carvery.
Around me all is chaos waiting to happen whilst no one hopes it will. They've crucified Euclid, Pythagoras, and there Newton defies gravity, suspended in mid theory, whilst Einstein plays dice and washes his hands of it, completely.
Things dart around like words flailing for sentences in the napalm of 'isms', like extras in Sci Fi movies bewailing the end with nigh conviction, like Thomas before the nails.
I am the wolf cub howling whilst a million Neros fiddle around me, I am Lazarus to mortality, the uncoy carp, the blind violently stroking a Glissando on an Empty Harp.

The video goes dark. Very dim lighting. It is before dawn. Illuminate a woman.

WOMAN It was love at first sight. I'd only snogged to Dean Freedman before or smooched to Chicago; when you're sixteen and hooked on patchouli you'd believe black was white if it drove a Ford Escort and knew all the words to Hotel California.
In school we'd squirm with lips like suckers; cheek to cheek, spots to spots, erupting with devotion, then

spend each evening at home slithering in the sauna of
our fumbled emotion.

We were the love doves of school, fated with the 'wws'
of post-pubescent admiration. We were young, free,
we loved the crack, maturing in each other like
Armagnac.

Then, one Summer he failed his exams and took a
career opportunity as a bottle washer in a pop factory,
and I was left alone in school, to mourn as if he'd gone
to war.

I was innocence's widow, tortured each night on the
rack of his maturity; who had I talked to, where had I
been, why had I done this or done that, said that or
done the other... And I submitted naively to his
inquisition. For he was in the big world now, and
called himself God... and who was I to doubt him?

A slow bell tolls as if it is a buoy at sea. It is being tolled by a dumb male character (Fergus). Two men, Eric and Emrys (the tramp bards) are also on stage.

EMRYS Ring that bell again, Quasimodo, and I'll ring a ding-a-ling 'round your ruddy neck! Oh God! Am I graced or disgraced?

ERIC What do you think?

EMRYS I think this isn't New Quay chip shop, you're not Debbie from Poppit Sands and I'm still as poor as a parasite on dog pwp?

ERIC You're right.

EMRYS Damn, I hate waking to poverty; it's like being slobbered on by Dobermans. Is there a world out there? Are you receiving me?

ERIC Too loud and too clear.

EMRYS Well it's not clear from where I am. From where I am it's as black as a Guinness bum. Tell me something Eric.

ERIC What?

EMRYS Where's the day gone?

ERIC It hasn't dawned yet, Emrys.

EMRYS Then it's still early.

ERIC Too early.

EMRYS How early?

ERIC As early as lug diggers.

EMRYS Oh God, I hate catching the worm! (*pause*) I was visited by an angel again, last night, Eric.

ERIC Again!

EMRYS Well, to be honest, I'm not sure.

ERIC What do you mean, you're not sure?

EMRYS It could have been a dream.

ERIC Were you awake at the time?

EMRYS   I couldn't tell, I was too drunk. It was after I'd drained the pubs dry down to the sea.

ERIC   There's no sea near here.

EMRYS   I was speaking metaphorically.

ERIC   What happened?

EMRYS   I was writing the night's saga upon some wall or other with the yellow ink of my mounting pen - etching a dada masterpiece which melted like trade unions in Winter - when I was caught in flagrante by an heavenly being.

ERIC   Nabbed by an angel in mid pissoir.

EMRYS   Exactly. I was sure it was an angel because only the divine would dare to be focused after stop tap. 'How dare you invade me lucidly at this ungodly hour!' I shouted. 'Haven't you got better things to do ?' 'Come with me' said the angel, 'and we'll fly and flutter from star to star.' 'Go and start a ruddy religion,' I said, 'I prefer my angels to pilot me to the bar'.

ERIC   And did it go away?

EMRYS   God knows. Oh God!

Emrys groans.

ERIC   What's wrong Emrys?

EMRYS   What's right you mean. Is half of my head over there?

ERIC   No.

EMRYS   Are you sure?

ERIC   Why do you ask?

EMRYS   I've got a splitting headache, I think a bit of my brain has slunk out like a wax ball overnight.

ERIC   Try blaming the beer.

EMRYS   As a rational man maybe I should. But, as an irrational poet, I rest my case. For beer is to bardd as bread is to butter; it is the force that drives culture through the furze. Beer is the manure of creativity. No beer, no beauty, simple as that. What do you reckon?

ERIC   Reckoning, my dear Emrys, is solely a post-meridian pastime. In the morning I'm just blind and bigoted.

EMRYS   I blame the chemicals that lace the ale.

ERIC   They are a sin.

EMRYS   The only sin in my book - the sin of bad beer, all else is forgivable. What do you think?

ERIC   I don't think before dawn.

EMRYS   So if it never dawned you'd never think.

ERIC   That's a horrible thought.

EMRYS   Think about it, Eric.

ERIC   I don't want to think about it.

EMRYS   Fair's fair. What a thought, eh!...no dawn?... like a note for the milkman - 'Sorry Ernie, no dawn today'. Now there's a sobering thought, I'm a judge already. No dawn, the ultimate cure for a hangover. Think about it and you could go mad, couldn't you?

ERIC   You could, it's why I...

EMRYS   ...don't think about it. Very wise. Because what if it never came? What if dawn never again cracked the horizon like a walnut at Christmas? What if we were to lie here for the rest of our lives, shivering underneath the arches waiting for the light, like an eternal Flanagan and Allen dreaming our dreams of a new day; two Tramp Bards dying in the dark. Now there's a thought and an half for you.

ERIC   I prefer not to think about it! OK.

EMRYS   Come to think about it, so do I.

Pause.

ERIC   The dawn will come, Emrys.

EMRYS   Are you sure?

ERIC   I hope to God it does.

EMRYS   But you don't believe in God, Eric.

ERIC   I don't care as long as God believes in me! I live in hope.

EMRYS   I hope so too. (*To dumb character - Fergus*) Fergus hopes so, not that Fergus would ruddy know what he's hoping for, silly bugger. You're a no-hoper, aren't you, Fergus? You wouldn't know hope if it came up to you and sucked your eyes out, would you, Fergus?

ERIC   I think that he'd see the point.

EMRYS   And see no more. God, can you imagine the eternal nightmare of darkness chewing the cud of your hope? Oh my God, can you imagine that?

ERIC   No, I can't!

EMRYS   Can't you?

ERIC   Of course I can. I just don't want to!

EMRYS   Why not? Imagining's your stock in trade. Call yourself a poet!

ERIC   I am a realist. I hate the surreal. I hate the perversion of sanity in the satanic mills of night; the skewering of my soul on the points of Dali's moustache.
I like daylight and the ethics of predictability; the smell of soldiers sweating on parade, the twitching of the hanged, the gaggling of the near-dead at funerals, the repulsion of it all.

EMRYS   You like that?

ERIC   Liking is irrelevant. I can cope with it, coping is the game, it's all we can hope for. It's our only hope.

Lights down. Video up.

HEAD	The atmosphere here is confused and vicious like a swarm of hornets mating on a Pollock canvas or Christmas at Holyhead when the ferry docks spew out the coagulated inebriates of a cross Celtic fraternity, who utilise every available wall as a pissoir al fresco. The hate is gangrenous and as thick as a Rottweiler's skull, so thick you couldn't cut it with a scythe. And the smell... a Pudding Lane mélange of acrid pus and the rotting sculptures of Paris Dadaismus; as stinking and putrid as a chicken plucker's fingernails teasing life as his hairy candle spurts and flails. This is Pandora's box; the venomed apple on the tree of life, inhabited by a myriad of infections and afflictions more revolting than the tongues of spaniels, slobbering under the milk starched crinolines of perverse etiquette. Listed in a nineteenth-century guide book, this box would share honours with industrial Llanelli; 'Not worth the detour, avoid it completely'.

Video off. Lights up on men. Fergus tolls a bell.

EMRYS	Deafen me three times before dawn and you'll be ringing bells in Atlantis!
ERIC	Emrys, why do you abuse him?
EMRYS	It's a sign of affection. To abuse him is to like him. If I didn't like him I'd be nice to him.
ERIC	That's perverse, Emrys.
EMRYS	It's a perverse world, Eric; a garden of earthly blight where night is dark and day more dark than night. A kinky nocturne where the only hope is poetry - the ultimate in beauty and creativity.

ERIC   What are you saying?

EMRYS   Do you believe that poetry could change the world?

ERIC   I believe only what I see, the world changes constantly; all poems change the world and the world changes poetry.

EMRYS   But what if there was one poem; one set of words, one glorious harmony of sound which had the power to change everything?

ERIC   Everything?

EMRYS   All the suffering.

ERIC   All life is suffering.

EMRYS   Don't be so 'realistic' Eric.

ERIC   I can't be anything else, I wear my reality on my sleeve like a custard stain.

EMRYS   That is a custard stain, mun.

ERIC   Qud erat demonstratum.

EMRYS   For God's sake Eric, listen. Imagine the most beautiful sound in the universe; the ultimate poem. A poem of such power that it can create and destroy; make day from night or kill like a Japanese Katzu. A poem of such force that not only is hearing it ecstasy but a spiritual satori. I live in hope that such a poem hasn't t been written.

ERIC	Why?
EMRYS	I'd like to write it. Pen the poem which would change the world.
ERIC	Your poetry couldn't change underwear.
EMRYS	At least I'm published!
ERIC	I'd rather be unpublished and forgotten than published in a journal with less circulation than angina.
EMRYS	I have attained immortality in print.
ERIC	It is immoral that you're printed.
EMRYS	You are just jealous, Eric.
ERIC	Of what?
EMRYS	Of what! Being poet of the week in a photocopied monthly, I'd rather be Tipexed to death.
EMRYS	Just Tipex out all your poetry, that would be less of a loss than being cured of leprosy.
ERIC	Pricked by the Welshman with the sharp-tongued wit.
EMRYS	There's more where that came from for I am a poet.
ERIC	A poet! You canker the term by association.
EMRYS	You talk through your rectum.
ERIC	I speak the speech trippingly from my tongue.

EMRYS   Your poetry is versified abomination.

ERIC   Your metre is measured in inches, your verse shoots itself in the foot.

EMRYS   Your...

ERIC   What?

EMRYS   Your.....What the hell rhymes with foot! Your poetry is crap, crap , crap, crap, crap!

ERIC   And yours is.........crapper.

A woman interrupts them.

WOMAN   Stop farting 'round like two flies in a box and give me an hand, will you ?

EMRYS   Did you hear that?

ERIC   I heard something.

EMRYS   It sounded like a voice.

ERIC   Then ignore it, it might lose itself.

WOMAN   For crying out loud!

ERIC   It is a voice!

EMRYS   A female voice!

ERIC   Oh my God! I haven't cleaned my teeth yet.

EMRYS   This is the Thames Embankment not the ruddy Ritz, Eric. This is the halitosised gutter, where dentists fear to tread. Relax. People who need a hand down here rarely smell your breath for reference.

WOMAN   For crying out loud, I am about to give birth here, now, in front of you...

ERIC   You can t do that.

WOMAN   Why not?

EMRYS   This is a public place.

ERIC   You can't drop litter.

EMRYS   We are not doctors, this is hardly a hospital.

ERIC   This is the Thames Embankment, we are Tramp Bards and the only thing we've given birth to is poetry...

WOMAN   I don't care if you've only given berth to trawlers in Hull harbour. My contractions are getting closer, for God's sake help me.

EMRYS   Oh God! Reality is my worst nightmare.

ERIC   I could think of worse.

EMRYS   You're right, so could I.

ERIC   I know you could.

EMRYS   How?

ERIC   I've heard your dreams.

EMRYS I've also heard yours.

WOMAN I don't care if you've both heard Tom Jones in concert. For Pete's sake help me!

ERIC   Is Pete the name of your child?

EMRYS What if it's a girl?

ERIC   She could be short for Petra.

EMRYS She could call it Petrol.

ERIC   Don't be so stupid.

EMRYS I'm not being stupid. I've heard of triplets in India called first gear, second gear, third gear.

ERIC   This is not India.

WOMAN This is an emergency. For God's sake!

EMRYS Is Pete God?

WOMAN My waters have broken.

EMRYS Send for a doctor!

ERIC   Send for a plumber!

WOMAN There's no time to send for anyone. Please! Though I'm loath to beg you, I implore you, please help me!

EMRYS   You're the social realist, you deal with it.

ERIC   You're Romantic, idealise it.

WOMAN   For God's sake, give me a hand!

ERIC   Sounds like an offer to perform manual labour.

EMRYS   I'd rather perform the Ring cycle by Wagner.

BOTH   Fergus, you get in there!

The dumb character is pushed under her skirt.

ERIC   What are you going to do?

EMRYS   I'll hold her hand ...

ERIC   I'll make the tea.

EMRYS   We haven't got any tea.

ERIC   Then I'll write the poetry... I can't look.

EMRYS   Neither can I.

WOMAN   God! Ah!... Ah!... I hope to God this is worth it!

She tightly squeezes Emrys' hand.

EMRYS   Aargh! I hope so too.

WOMAN   Ah!

Lights down. Video on.

The image appears on her skirt – as if in her womb.

HEAD	Here is the city of woe; the city of eternal pain, not the place where I'd wish to be. Unfortunately, here I am - an exquisite cadaver dwelling in hell, hoping to hell I can get out of here. For here, reality is more terrifying than death in a toilet, so I close my eyes and dance my surreal nocturnes upon the filter of my dreams. And one dream in particular circles inevitably, round and round my mind, like a Tibetan prayer wheel, or the tension in a football derby. I am a child, walking down a corridor carrying a crate of mothers' milk in those little third pint bottles that fed a generation. It's raining sunshine on the rhododendrons outside, blinding me with a blow-torch glare. Of a sudden, I stop and drop the milk which smashes in scarlet upon the floor and stare straight ahead of me. I daren't look down because I'm convinced that I'm naked as if my clothes had dissolved like rice paper on the tongue. And one question runs round my mind girdling my anima - Am I male or am I female? If I looked down what would I see? Eventually I gather my wind in my palms and look, and I see that I've still got my clothes on and I'm none the wiser. From within I hear the laughter of Duchamp and Picabia!

The dumb character rings the bell violently from under the skirt. The lights go up.

ERIC	I can see the dawn. Thank God!

EMRYS	I can't see a ruddy thing, I'm blinded by pain.

ERIC	All life is pain. Pain is the reassurance of life itself.

EMRYS	Then at the moment I must be more alive than ten toddlers on Tartazine.
ERIC	No pain, no gain, Emrys.
EMRYS	What the hell am I gaining?
ERIC	An understanding.
EMRYS	I'd rather gain ten stone and wire my mouth.
WOMAN	Just wire your mouth!

She makes birth sounds. Emrys and Woman crescendo.

WOMAN	Aargh! It's coming! It's coming! Aargh!
ERIC	Fergus! Is it a boy? Is it a girl?
EMRYS	He can't answer you, he can't speak. He can ring his bell.
ERIC	Good thinking. Ring your bell, Fergus; once for a boy, twice for a girl.

Fergus rings his bell three times. The Tramp Bards look puzzled at each other. They pull the skirt aside and Fergus backs out holding a box.

EMRYS	What a beautiful...beautiful... baby!
ERIC	It's a box!
EMRYS	Sh!

ERIC   What was his father, a portakabin? Smack it!

EMRYS   Where?

ERIC   On its bum.

EMRYS   A box hasn't got a bum.

ERIC   It must have.

EMRYS   Where?

ERIC   I don't know. Behind its bits.

EMRYS   What bits?

ERIC   The bits between its legs!

EMRYS   For God's sake, a box hasn't got legs! What the hell! For crying out...

ERIC   If you must swear cover its ears!

EMRYS   Cover its ears! I can't even find its head!

ERIC   Has it got eyes?

EMRYS   Not that I can see.

ERIC   A mouth?

EMRYS   The poor dab's born to be hungry.

ERIC   Where do you put a nappy?

WOMAN   How is my baby?

ERIC   Interesting.

ERIC   Hell's teeth, man. Are you going to tell her or shall I?

EMRYS   Is that a rhetorical question?

ERIC   Of course.

EMRYS   Oh thank you. For an atheist, Eric, you sure know all the tricks.

ERIC   My dear Emrys, I've listened to the cream of the bishoprics.

EMRYS   I bet you have.

WOMAN   Pass me my child.

EMRYS   I'm not... sure... whether that's a... a good idea.

WOMAN   Why?

EMRYS   Are you really ready for the most monumental moment of your life?

WOMAN   What would you suggest? A quick perm and set?

EMRYS   Not exactly.

WOMAN   Then what?

EMRYS   How's your Greek History?

WOMAN Fact or mythology?

EMRYS I was thinking more Geometrically.

WOMAN For God's sake, stop talking in circles and deal squarely with me.

EMRYS Well...?

WOMAN ...Dora...

EMRYS ...Dora, I don't quite know how to put this.

WOMAN Square on your tongue and spit it out.

EMRYS Sometimes one must be cruel to be kind.

WOMAN What's that got to do with my child?

EMRYS We wouldn't want you to mother a runt.

WOMAN Let me decide who or what I want to mother.

ERIC But you might be disappointed.

WOMAN My child could never disappoint me. Only I could disappoint my baby. For nine months I have felt invaded by an Alien; nurturing a life which has just exploded from within. I have seen my body mutating, playing guinea pig to nature's plastic surgery, changing the shape of my body completely. I have basked in contentment like a mud-caked elephant, glowing with the pride of each blissful moment.
For nine months I have been both bored and released by the advances of an upturned husband, grinning like

a joy-rider at the depth of 'his' achievement.
This same man who appropriated everything that I was; my love, my life, my hope, my dreams solely for a chance at immortality. Never again will a man do that to me. So give me my child!!

She rips free from her dress and the Tramp Bards rush to give her her child.

ERIC   Here, take it!

WOMAN   Thankyouohmybaby! .... Oh my gorgeous baby, you are purest beauty; a beauty that will pass through life and will let life pass through it. That is poetry, the true art of creation.

She drools over her child.

EMRYS   Oh indeed, the purest beauty is a beautiful baby...

ERIC   She hasn't noticed that her child's a box.

EMRYS   Beauty's in the eye of the beholder.

ERIC   Do you think that she needs glasses?

EMRYS   No, but we need a serious talk....

They huddle in a corner.
Fergus is captivated by 'Hope'.

EMRYS   Did you hear what she said, Eric?

ERIC   What I heard and what I saw were conflicted like the spine-smashing tackle of a rugby-playing pacifist. She called her child the purest beauty but a box is a box is a box.

EMRYS   Like a coffin's a coffin ?

ERIC   Exactly; an object of utility. There's no beauty in function, there's just necessity.

EMRYS   Not necessarily, Eric. You see, she went on to say something more.

ERIC   I closed my ears to the metaphor.

EMRYS   Well, had you kept them open, you would have heard her say that her child, her box, her '... beauty, will pass through life and life will pass through it". She called her child poetry, poetry mark you. The 'true embodiment of creation'.

ERIC   She said that?

EMRYS   That's what I believe she said.

ERIC   Then it might not be true.

EMRYS   I believe it to be true and if I believe that it's true, then it must be true, because my truth is as valid as anybody's.

ERIC   Really?

EMRYS   Either my truth is truth or I'm truly mad.

ERIC   Well...

EMRYS   Don't answer that.

ERIC   Answer what?

EMRYS   Do you believe in the synchronicity of events?

ERIC   In everything there is an element of chance.

EMRYS   I'm not talking chance, I'm talking destiny. We were meant to meet this woman.

ERIC   Dear Emrys, we just happened to be here, she chanced upon us.

EMRYS   You can't be a Camus and a Kierkegaard, Eric. Chance or destiny - what's it to be?

ERIC   Oh my God, we haven't even had breakfast yet and already we've witnessed birth and analysed the placenta of its philosophy. Why can't you give me a simple choice, say between croissant or toast?

EMRYS   We've got no food, we've only got words. Chance or destiny, which is it to be?

ERIC   Neither, both exist simultaneously.

EMRYS   How can they?

ERIC   Chance is a possibility, fate the probability. The probable and the possible co-exist like night and day, toryism and sanity, black and white, chance and destiny; both sides of a chaotic tiddly-wink tossing towards the pot.
        I'm a realist, Emrys, and I realise that there is no

reality, there is just the probability that it possibly exists.

EMRYS   Don't whip me with rhetoric, Eric. We were destined to witness the birth of her child.

ERIC   ... Her box ...

EMRYS   ...No ordinary box. That box is the key to creation - within it lies the ultimate poetical perfection; the perfect poem is crystallised within that box.

ERIC   Have you proof of this?

EMRYS   I have a kismetic feeling... Right here!

ERIC   That's just hunger.

EMRYS   I know the difference between hunger and a hunch; call it fatalism, call it instinct...

ERIC   ... I call it crazy ...

EMRYS   ... But I think that inside her box is the ultimate in versified creation; the perfect set of sounds, the enigmatic sonics of life itself. I want to possess that box, I feel that I am fated to possess it. And by possessing that box I will possess the ultimate poem and by possessing the ultimate poem, I will have ultimate power.

ERIC   You don't want much, do you?

EMRYS   I want your help to get hold of the box.

ERIC   I'm not so sure.

EMRYS   Come on Eric...

Woman interrupts them.

WOMAN   So you two are Tramp Bards?

EMRYS   We are the poets of penury.

WOMAN   And Fergus?

EMRYS   He's just an idiot; cannon fodder in less interesting times.

WOMAN   Things are hard on you?

EMRYS   Things are always hard on us, hard on us is not our problem. Problems could be hard as Latin or hard as Fonteyn's bunions, they wouldn't bother us. The muse is our comfort, it warms the cockles of our hearts.

WOMAN   Then what is your problem?

EMRYS   Our problem is when things become hard for other people. Then they become impossible for us. You see poetry, like arson, is a product with a vicious, delicate beauty. But you cannot quantify beauty or measure the worth of ideals. They are elusive abstracts that are first to hit the fan when the effluent flies. In a market economy, poetry is about as valuable as principles. But we still write, what else could we do? We are the musing bemused picking our way across Crib Goch in the dark. We are burnished shields charting the reflection of life.

ERIC   I prefer to chart reality, but, at the moment I must admit, it's a bit too real to digest.

EMRYS So you see, all in all, we're going through a bit of a sticky patch. We have had a glorious past and we are hopeful for the future.

ERIC   But for the time being, our luck has ebbed and we are two beached whales singing laments to the sea.

EMRYS What about you?

WOMAN Me!

ERIC   What's your history?

WOMAN I am a dumb woman who didn't finish her education. In my town it was bad manners to have more brain than your boyfriend, so I bowed to the pressure and bowed out of school and trained as a dental receptionist. One Saturday afternoon I had my wisdom teeth extracted gratis…

EMRYS Torture was a perk of the job, was it?

WOMAN It was a vital part of the business, the locked jaw grin of advertising. My mouth was a flossed billboard capped to attract a clientele; bridged to bring in the bucks.

EMRYS And did it work?

WOMAN My choppers opened fetes, they were the talk of the town and more admired than a Harley Davidson cruising through Swansea as the sun goes down.

> Anyway, on the day in question, after the operation, I rendezvoused in Brachi's caff with my boyfriend and over a bowl of faggots he leant over, reeking of cooked flesh and cappuccino, and proposed to me. 'Will you marry me or what?' he said, butter freezing in his mouth.

EMRYS   And what did you say?

WOMAN   What could I say? My novocained tongue attempted to formulate the word 'What!' but he took my slobbering attempts at speech as affirmative and rang my parents pronto to be the first with the good news. That night I chose to remain invisible because I didn't want to hurt anybody. My mother cried, my father transferred his property and the bargain was struck and sucked on the bitter dregs of a four pack.

EMRYS   Scandalous!

WOMAN   I felt like a young Indian bride about to jump onto the pyre; like a victim in the fractured moment before a crash or a blue lobster over the dyeing steam.
I was eighteen and I wanted to scream against the travesty, but I was taught to serve and I stood dumb, a silent woman cursing the bones of their curriculum.

ERIC   So you got married?

WOMAN   Yes, and domesticity vapourised into condensed clouds of resentment. One morning I woke up to my husband's imprint in the bed beside me. I didn't hug the pillow or caress the sheets, I read them, like 'Chinganchook' testing the coals of a long-dead fire. When did my husband come home last night? I cursed that he had and wondered what time he left that morning. I was desperately angling for a divorce motive, you see, fishing for an excuse and netting red herrings from beneath the duvet. In a mutinous mood I got up and hissed off to the toilet where malice was well rewarded. For there, like sunburn blisters on a soon-to-be cancerous back, droplets of his master's urine shone quicksilver upon the throne. The sod hadn't lifted the toilet seat again. How often had I begged him to do this! How often had I lodged my formal complaint in emotional triplicate? That was it, I'd found my motive and I wasn't going to hang around for explanations - no way was I going to sit in that man's piss any longer. So I took all the major credit cards and fled, ending up here.

ERIC How long ago was that?

WOMAN Long enough for him to have realised his true loss and cancelled my credit cards.

ERIC And will he come looking for you?

WOMAN He'll come unfortunately. He'll appear like pimples before a date. But he won't come for me, he'll come for immortality.

She motions to the box. Emrys takes this in.

EMRYS Your baby.

WOMAN Yeah, my baby.

EMRYS Your baby is immortal...

WOMAN   In his eyes, yes. He's convinced that my baby is his passport to the everlasting; by fathering a child he will live eternally .

EMRYS   Immortality! How sick can a man get, I ask you?

ERIC   He seems mad. Mad!

EMRYS   As mad as marbles. If he comes, don't worry, we'll protect you, won't we Eric?

ERIC   We will.

EMRYS   We will! You see, I have a great feeling that it was destiny that drew us together to be bonded in a moment of pain and midwifery. We were fated to be mutually beneficial.

WOMAN   I don't think so. I want nothing from you; least of all your patronising patronage. I've just shuffled off one macho coil and I don't need Tweedle Dum and Dee to protect me. Don't worry about us, we'll get by just fine on our own.

She goes to go.

EMRYS   Dora! It's as mad as Pound's Cantos out there. Stay with us, at least until you gain some strength.

WOMAN   I am stronger without you.

EMRYS   But no man is an island, Dora.

WOMAN   I am not a man.

EMRYS   But Dora, think of your child.

WOMAN   Believe me, I am.

ERIC   Please stay, Dora!!

WOMAN   Aargh!

She crumples in pain. Eric goes to her.

ERIC   Are you all right?

WOMAN   I'm very weak.

ERIC   Can I get you anything?

WOMAN   (*reluctantly*) Yes, some water.

ERIC   (*he has a flask*) Here we are.

WOMAN   Thank you.

ERIC   Please don't thank me.

WOMAN   I would like to.

ERIC   There's no need.

WOMAN   I want to.

ERIC   It's unneccessary...

WOMAN   Just allow me to thank you with dignity!

ERIC   I'm...

WOMAN   Don't say sorry, just leave me be.

ERIC   I'm your right hand man if you need me.

WOMAN   Yes.

Eric smiles and goes back to Emrys. The poets huddle.

EMRYS   Excellent, Eric, I have never ever witnessed a more stunning deployment of mock sincerity in all my born. The longing tones of your pleading please pimpled my pimples.
        Personally, I thought we'd blown it, I could see my hopes floating by like fly-by-night art movements and then you jumped in and rescued the day, with manners fit to kiss a Pope's ring.

ERIC   Yes, well...

EMRYS   Accept my gratitude as a fellow-traveller, dispossessed of all save the stars. Thank you, thank you, thank you. Though I'm penniless...

ERIC   You're not in my debt.

EMRYS   No name it, anything.

ERIC   I don't want anything.

EMRYS   You must want something? You must have a desire, a need (*Eric thinks*). How about a share in the royalties of my only published poem?

ERIC   I don't want money.

EMRYS	I didn't get money. I'm offering you half a thank-you letter.
ERIC	No, thank you.
EMRYS	Fair's fair. What if I write an epic poem glorifying your life and triumphs - something Aneirinesque. It won't be that long, but it's the principle that counts.
ERIC	It does?
EMRYS	So a mention in dispatches is OK then?
ERIC	No.
EMRYS	No!
ERIC	No. I want something more than the plastic convenience of your fast food words, Emrys. I want to barter more than platitudes.
EMRYS	You want a deal?
ERIC	Yes.
EMRYS	But the only thing I have to swap are anecdotes.
ERIC	I want neither news nor history.
EMRYS	Then deal on the nail.
ERIC	I want to stake my claim to beauty.
EMRYS	You want the box!

ERIC   (*reassuringly*) No.

EMRYS   What a relief, for a moment then...

ERIC   ... I want its mother.

EMRYS   You want Dora?

ERIC   (*nods*)

EMRYS   Kiss my corns! Hook line and sinker!

ERIC   Yes.

EMRYS   For Dora?

ERIC   Yes.

EMRYS   Oh my God, forgive him, he's fallen in lust.

ERIC   In love...

EMRYS   Don't walk before you can crawl, Eric. You have fallen in lust... with Dora! What can I say? Throw me a simile! I am at sea without a metaphor. This is indeed a heaven-sent opportunity.

ERIC   You said there was no chance-only destiny.

EMRYS   Exactly! Fate rears its Vesuvian head, Eric; each to his own beauty! Your beauty created of love and mine of ecstatic poetry. Your dream is Dora, my dream is the box, together we could realise the flesh and blood of our dreams. So I agree to a deal; I'll take the box, you take its mother.

ERIC   OK.

EMRYS   And no toe treading of one on the other.

ERIC   It's a deal.

EMRYS   Excellent.

They spit and shake.

ERIC   OK, so what's the plan?

EMRYS   God knows, but it's time to think of one.

Lights down on the two men and up on the woman.

WOMAN   There's a good baby, mammy's beautiful baby, as beautiful as the knowing beauty of a silent k. You know mammy loves you. You do know, don't you? I feel that you know everything though you don't let on. You lie there observing the world melting like minutes on a Sunday and you say nothing; not a sound out of you. You're a full vessel oozing brain and promise... My Promise. Dear Promise, you are my living hope.

She hums and rocks the baby. Lights down. Video on.

HEAD   Some nights ago, I held rather a fraught discussion with a few anti-social blights upon the nature of art. The Moth of Homicidal Violence claimed, by tracing its roots from the automatic writings of Dadaism, that Football hooliganism, and in particular the cathartic etchings of Stanley, are the unfiltered expressions of pure art. At knifepoint, and not wishing to disagree, I held my hands up in submission only for them to be severed and consumed by famine, who in between sucking the marrow from my metatarsals stated emphatically that 'Art should be edible or not at all'. Whereupon he threw up and sucked his sick back up through a straw.

Withdrawing to the comparative safety of the corner, I ventured that life is like a painting by Seurat; the memory of a zillion stars on the Mayfly wings of the night. An infinity of instants creating an effect - stand too close and you'll see a blur, stand back and you must be dead; for only Death can survey the whole history of a human on the pointilled canvas of its soul. Whereupon prejudice who had listened calculatingly to the whole debate leant over and proceeded to blind me.

Video off. Lights up.

WOMAN (*Humming*)

EMRYS Dear Dora.

WOMAN What do you want of me?

EMRYS I'd like a short word.

WOMAN Keep it brief.

EMRYS I'll try. We live in a new Federal Europe where walls of misunderstanding are being demolished to make way for drive-through Macdonalds; a world where porn and politics are transmitted simultaneously, blurring the boundaries between both.

WOMAN   Get on with it.

EMRYS   As poets we are dedicated to communication and we feel that we are, in some small way, contributing to the developing dialogue. It is sad therefore that a misunderstanding has arisen between us this morning.

WOMAN   Sad but predictable.

EMRYS   Indeed, it is a sorry state that man can communicate with man on the moon but not with the woman besides him.

WOMAN   Predictably sad.

EMRYS   But you must remember that no poem worth its ink was written in a day. We are products of our upbringing, still prone to smatterings of sexism...

WOMAN   Smatterings! You threw the whole ink pot!

EMRYS   Perhaps we did, but by admitting our errors we are able to change.

WOMAN   Are you?

EMRYS   We were only thinking of your welfare.

WOMAN   Were you?

EMRYS   It's an urban jungle out there, Dora, populated by all sorts of Thatcherite sub-species who would kill you for the price of a Pimms and lemonade. We only had your best interests in mind, we are after all in the same dingy, different oars, same seas of change. If we rowed together we could make the promised land.

WOMAN   Just jump off the boat!

EMRYS   Dora fach, please. This morning you delivered hope into the world...

WOMAN   And what are you delivering, 'the Sermon on the Mount'?

EMRYS   Not delivering but appealing for a little forgiveness and co-operation.

WOMAN   I've told you once, I don't need your help.

EMRYS   For the sake of your child?

WOMAN   I'm fully capable of taking care of my baby.

EMRYS   But are you? It's a man-eat-man world out there.

WOMAN   And I'm strictly vegetarian. What are you trying to do, frighten me, make me feel guilty? Don't hoist me by the petard of my own gender. I'm fed up of posing pouches telling me what I can and what I cannot do.

ERIC   I'm only trying to help.

WOMAN   Help who?

EMRYS   All of us; you, me, Fergus, Eric and your baby.

WOMAN   Why?

EMRYS   Why? Because I'm an altruistic kinda guy, that's why. I want to help you.

WOMAN   What about Eric?

EMRYS   He...

WOMAN   Let him speak for himself.

Eric has a brainstorm.

ERIC   How do you love a fascist sympathiser? / With a sledgehammer through his head / 'till his brains slump out and proclaim he's dead? Oh my God I said the wrong thing!

WOMAN   Is he published?

EMRYS   Not yet.

WOMAN   Thought not.

EMRYS   He means well.

WOMAN   What does he mean?

EMRYS   What Eric means is... How do you love man? With love and truth until he acknowledges the paradox of his gender?

WOMAN   You meant that?

ERIC   Yes.

WOMAN   And you want to help me?

ERIC   Yes.

WOMAN   Honestly?

ERIC   Yes...yes...yes...yes.

EMRYS   He is afflicted, for love is an affliction. Eric is sick, sick with the tree frog poison of Cupid's prick. He wants to help you because he loves you. Don't you, Eric?

ERIC   Yes.

WOMAN   He is in love with me?

EMRYS   Yes.

WOMAN   Honestly.

EMRYS   He loves you, honestly.

WOMAN   'He loves you honestly' like a pre-pubescent playground threat where lips are more than a penny. 'He loves you honestly', has 'he' no tongue, if he has no tongue what good is he for kissing? So 'he loves' does he. Has he ever loved before, so that he can he compare me to anyone that he once thought he loved, and has since realised that he never even cared for? 'He loves you'; the 'you' being me. I don't know who I am so how does he know who I am, for him to love me... 'He loves you honestly'. What is honesty bar the mutual agreement to accept a reality, regardless of whether it's true or not. Eric, don't suffocate love in the killing jar of your vocabulary until you can tell me honestly that you love yourself, then tell me that you love me.

ERIC   But I do love you, honestly!

WOMAN	All of me?
ERIC	Yes.
WOMAN	You haven't shown much affection for my Promise.
ERIC	That's because that's Emrys' department.
EMRYS	What!
WOMAN	And what does that make me? Harrods? Departmentalised woman. I've heard of divide and conquer but this is absurd.
ERIC	No, you're jumping at the wrong end of the stick.
WOMAN	Not jumping, but hopping.
ERIC	Hoping?
WOMAN	Hopping mad. How dare you carve me up like Bosnia. I am no cake to be eaten by the poor. You called my husband sick, he was positively compos mentis compared to you three. What part was Fergus allocated, my voice! God, you three disgust me... Don't worry, baby, mammy will protect you from the poets of penury.
EMRYS	Dora, please don't misunderstand Eric, he didn't mean what he said or what I mean is, he said what he meant but it meant something different to you... You know what I mean.
DORA	No, I don't know what the hell anybody means any more.

ERIC What I mean is this... words are sprung traps in the minefield of social discourse.

WOMAN What!

EMRYS Words can be misinterpreted. What Eric meant when he said that your baby was my department was that... I feel a warmth towards all children, Dora. A Santa Claus complex towards kids, and towards your child in particular.

WOMAN Pull the other.

EMRYS No, seriously. I am a whiz with kids.

WOMAN I can't see you with children, Emrys.

EMRYS I love 'em.

WOMAN All of them?

EMRYS Crêches full of them.

WOMAN Why?

EMRYS Why? That's a very difficult question...

WOMAN I bet it is.

EMRYS No, you misunderstand me, it's hard to put my finger on why I particularly like 'em.

WOMAN Try.

EMRYS Well, I especially like their little minds that can see red trees where we see green, and hope where we see despair.

WOMAN You despair?

EMRYS Oh, I do.

WOMAN Do you?

EMRYS You see, I once had a child... a baby boy, name of Sam, I say had, as opposed to have, because he's six now and I haven't seen him since he was... oh about four weeks old.

WOMAN I'm sorry, I didn't know.

EMRYS That's OK. He was a little dwt when I saw him last; before his mother took him away and made things difficult for us to see each other. Anyway, Sam's mother's got a new boyfriend now, and I guess Sam calls him dad...

WOMAN Too bad.

EMRYS No, no, no, no it's the way of the world. There's always something to regret, hope for, desire...

WOMAN Promise is all I could ever hope for...

EMRYS Promise!

WOMAN Yes, that's her name.

EMRYS Her!

WOMAN Hadn't you noticed?

EMRYS I didn't like to look.

WOMAN She's my hope.
EMRYS Hope of what?

WOMAN Happiness.

EMRYS Whose happiness?

WOMAN Everybody's.

EMRYS Oh.

WOMAN She is perfection.

EMRYS As perfect as the purest poetry?

WOMAN I guess so.

EMRYS Really... what did I tell you, Eric! May I?

WOMAN You'd like to hold her?

EMRYS Just for a second, is that OK?

WOMAN Not for long.

EMRYS No. Thank you.

The baby is handed over.

EMRYS (*makes baby noises*) Pretty Promise... Pretty Promise.

WOMAN   She's not a parrot, Emrys.

EMRYS   Sorry, Dora. Hello, Promise, it's Uncle Emrys here. Give me a little smile then, c'mon, smile for Uncle Emrys. Look at that. Look at that. She's smiling, she likes me.

WOMAN   It's probably wind.

Eric takes Emrys aside. The woman is nervous.

ERIC   I never knew you had a son.

EMRYS   I haven't.

ERIC   You haven't!

EMRYS   No.

ERIC   Then you...

EMRYS   Lied, yeah. It's all part of the plan, Eric, part of the plan.

ERIC   We have a plan!

EMRYS   The plan of improvisation.

ERIC   You can't plan improvisation.

EMRYS   But improvisation can be a plan. Leave yourself open to the infinite possibilities and the miraculous could happen. Just play on.

WOMAN   What are you two scheming?

EMRYS   Not scheming but admiring the beauty of your child. She looks just like you, Dora.

WOMAN   Do you think so?

EMRYS   What do you think, Eric?

ERIC   Well...

EMRYS   It's post meridian, improvise, man.

Emrys hands the child over to Eric.

ERIC   Oh yes, yes. Promise is a beautiful baby. She has your eyes, Dora.

WOMAN   I thought maybe more the nose.

ERIC   Yes, you're right there, more the nose than the eyes, and her mouth...

WOMAN   A bottle-washer's mouth.

ERIC   Hardly worth a mention at all.

WOMAN   Exactly. I endured nine months of pain and discomfort for her to be born with his mouth. Every time I'll look at my baby I'll see his mocking lips like a pair of chiding magpies; every time I feed her I'll be sucked by the lips of a toilet seat wetter, I'd rather be boiled in butter... and do you know what he wanted to call her?

ERIC   No, sorry.

WOMAN   Don't be sorry, he should be sorry not you. He

wanted to call her Rwmania... Rwmania Sodapop Evans.

ERIC Why?

WOMAN Why, because he was a bottle-washer, that's why.

ERIC Rwmania Sodapop Evans?

WOMAN Mmm. Rwmania after the guest house where Promise was conceived. Damn stupid name for a two-bit guest house, Rwmania - I couldn't wait to get away from there.

ERIC And Sodapop...

WOMAN Sodapop was a fit of company loyalty - he figured that he'd be able to stall his inevitable redundancy with a brand-named baby.

ERIC And did he?

WOMAN Does plastic melt?

ERIC And Evans?

WOMAN A family name.

ERIC His family?

WOMAN Yes.

ERIC Rwmania Sodapop Evans!

WOMAN Damn stupid name, isn't it?

EMRYS   And what of Promise?

WOMAN   It is a name full of hope, Emrys.

EMRYS   Hope! Sounds like a ruddy schoolyard death sentence if you ask me.

WOMAN   Then what would you call her?

EMRYS   If I were you I'd call her Failure.

WOMAN   No wonder your wife left you.

EMRYS   Failure! A name without pressure, then every small gain would be a triumph, instead of every small setback a disaster.

ERIC   Don't be such a downer, Emrys. He can be one hell of a pessimist.

EMRYS   I take after my grandmother's legs.

ERIC   Then take your varicosed morals somewhere else. Promise is a lovely name, Dora.

WOMAN   Promise is my hope; the only hope that I've ever had in my whole life.

EMRYS   What about her life?

WOMAN   Promise is my baby! And no soda-popping bottle-washer or poet of penury is going to dictate to me what I should or should not call her.

EMRYS   I'm sorry, I shouldn't have spoken.

WOMAN   You shouldn't have. She is the paradigm of creation. I have named her, and she is mine.

EMRYS   Well...

WOMAN   Leave it!

ERIC   Please, Emrys.

EMRYS   OK.

ERIC   Sometimes Emrys can be two lines short of a sonnet. For God's sake, have some feelings man.

EMRYS   It's all part of the plan, Eric, part of the plan...

Emrys backs off.

WOMAN   Eric.

ERIC   Yes?

WOMAN   She likes you.

ERIC   Do you think so?

WOMAN   I can tell.

ERIC   How?

Woman points to the box.

WOMAN   That's a smile.

ERIC   I like her too, Dora.

Eric quickly returns the box.

EMRYS   You're in there, Eric...

ERIC   Do you think so?

EMRYS   I can see it now, Dora and Eric, the perfect couple; like yoghurt and thrush.

ERIC   So you think that I have a chance?

EMRYS   More than a chance, a certainty.

ERIC   A certainty... Is that good?

EMRYS   It's positively advantageous to our plan.

ERIC   So you think that she likes me.

EMRYS   Damn right, man! But before you flip your lid in the kleenexed clouds, we have a deal, remember.

ERIC   Don't worry, I haven't forgotten.

EMRYS   You'd better not. I've sacrificed the attraction that she obviously felt for me, in order that you might gain her affection. I played her along then withdrew my love, and as she reeled from my rejection she transferred her attentions to the surrogate you. And now it is you that she loves, thanks to me.

ERIC   Thank you.

EMRYS   Don't thank me vacuously, secure me the box.

ERIC   How?

EMRYS Call yourself a poet, mun.

ERIC   I am a poet.

EMRYS Then use your imagination.

Emrys pushes Eric towards the woman.

ERIC   Dora!

WOMAN Yes?

ERIC   Emrys says he's very sorry if he's offended you.

WOMAN For a poet he should choose his words better.

ERIC   At times perhaps he should. At other times it's his exuberance which sometimes comes up trumps.

WOMAN Well, he won't trump me. I don't trust his intentions.

ERIC   Neither do I.

WOMAN I'm not sure whether I trust yours either.

ERIC   But Dora, I don't want any harm to come to Promise.

WOMAN We don't intend to get hurt.

ERIC   Have you ever intended to catch flu?

WOMAN No.

ERIC   Then please... listen to me. Baptise Promise as soon as possible.

WOMAN   Baptise Promise! Why?

ERIC   As a protection against those who would wish to harm you. At any minute your husband could whirlwind 'round the corner in a shaft of testosterone. You can't waste an instant.

WOMAN   True, I've wasted too long.

ERIC   Then baptise your child.

WOMAN   It's such a waste of time and water.

ERIC   But once baptised Promise will be legally yours. You will have named her and by naming her no one will be able to take her away from you.

WOMAN   You're right. One small ceremony.

ERIC   One ceremony is all a man needs and then it's misery for eternity. Fight ceremony with ceremony. Baptise Promise immediately.

WOMAN   It does seem for the best.

ERIC   It is your only hope... Let me talk to Emrys.

WOMAN   Why Emrys?

ERIC   He's an expert in such matters.

WOMAN   Sorry. I don't trust him.

ERIC   Don't trust him, just use him. Once you've named Promise, he will be powerless over you both.

WOMAN   I don t know, he's only a poet.

ERIC   And a priest.

WOMAN   He's a priest?

ERIC   And a drunk, he's a very talented man. He's been pulpitted and published...

WOMAN   But mostly paralytic.

ERIC   Maybe, but he is qualified?

WOMAN   How qualified?

ERIC   As qualified as any man.

WOMAN   That's what worries me.

ERIC   Trust me.

WOMAN   Why should I?

ERIC   I.... respect you.

WOMAN   In my book that's a good enough reason not to.

ERIC   Emrys!

EMRYS   What?

ERIC   We need your services.

EMRYS   Which kind?

ERIC   Ecclesiastic.

EMRYS   Spiritual or ceremonial?

ERIC   Ceremonial.

EMRYS   Is it a funeral ... a wedding? I'm very good at weddings.

WOMAN   Is there a difference between the two?

EMRYS   Only in the ceremony.

ERIC   Neither, Dora was wondering about baptism.

EMRYS   Baptism! What an amazing synchronicity. I have just been sitting here, hungry for chocolate locusts covered in honey, wondering why I craved such a Baptist's feast.

ERIC   It is destiny.

EMRYS   From the mouths of babes, it must be. Would I be right in presuming that it is Promise that is to be baptised?

ERIC   You would.

EMRYS   And that you are enquiring as to whether I could officiate?

WOMAN   You are.

EMRYS   Then my dear Dora, let me assure you that the honour will be mine. Now, as there seems to be an urgency let's get this over with quickly, shall we? Hand me Promise, Dora. Give her to me... Come on, we can get this over with very quickly if you'll just hand her over... Put her in my arms, entrust her to me... Come on Dora, give her to me...

WOMAN   No!

EMRYS   (*threateningly*) Time is getting on, Dora. The sun's going down and at any moment your husband could come 'round the corner.

WOMAN   Don't pressure me, I'll have to think about it!

The woman leaves them. The poets scheme.

EMRYS   Damn sterling work Eric, the route to a man's heart is through his stomach, the route to a woman's is through her child; for a realist you're a romantic dynamo... Da iawn, boy... What's wrong?

ERIC   Sorry, Emrys, the deal's off.

EMRYS   The deal stays! I will possess the perfect poem contained within her box and you will help me.

ERIC   That's not a box, it's her child.

EMRYS   It's a box.

ERIC   It's her child.

EMRYS   It's a box, you said so yourself.

ERIC	Maybe, but it's her truth.
EMRYS	It's also my truth.
ERIC	The box contains all her promise.
EMRYS	As it contains mine.
ERIC	I don't want to see her hope destroyed, Emrys.
EMRYS	I don't want to destroy anything, I want to create. Within that box is 'the ultimate beauty'- those were her words, 'the most perfect poem known to man'. I want to possess that poem and become the apotheosis of a poet. I will have that box.
ERIC	I won't let you.
EMRYS	Iwanhwsami... What is wrong with you? We were the poets of penury, the tramp bards, we've consecrated our lives to the muse.
ERIC	I have found something more valuable than poetry, Emrys.
EMRYS	What's more valuable than poetry?
ERIC	Love.
EMRYS	Oh for God's sake.
ERIC	It is the ultimate truth, Emrys.

Emrys pulls out a knife.

EMRYS   Look, you wouldn't know love if it came up and French-kissed you with a knife. We have a deal, remember. I will have that box. I will name it and having named it, I will have power over it, then I will possess it. The perfect poem will be mine. Wise up, Eric, how dare you supersede the muse with lust. Poetry is the purest creativity; the essence of life itself!

ERIC   Love is the essence of life. I know that now. Great poets have cried for it, died for it and written about it. Poetry is merely the reflection of it.

EMRYS   Rubbish, an artist should live and die for his art; catch TB, starve, freeze, make love, drink himself stupid, drug a stupor; any experience to make him feel closer to the essence of things. Love is just another pint of Guinness polluting the Irish sea. Eric, you were once a poet and eclectic. Now you're just pathetic.

ERIC   You're the pathetic one, Emrys.

EMRYS   Eric....

ERIC   (*to Woman*) Could I please...

EMRYS   Eric! Remember our deal.

ERIC   All deals are off.

EMRYS   Eric!

ERIC   Off, Emrys!

Eric takes the woman into a corner.

ERIC	Dora.
WOMAN	I'm thinking, Eric, what do you want?
ERIC	Can I have a quick word, please?
WOMAN	Another one. Your quick words are turning into chapters, Eric...
ERIC	...When I was a child...
WOMAN	...And your chapters into a biography.
ERIC	I'll come straight to the point. I'm from a privileged background; crusts were always cut off my soldiers, skin never allowed to form on my cocoa, and once when a snake stood over my cot in Burma, mesmerising the silver-spooned infant within...
WOMAN	Yes yes, look, time is of the essence, Eric. I'm sorry to rush you but my husband could arrive at any second, it was you who said so yourself.
ERIC	Please, Dora, please! Just give me a little of your time.
WOMAN	OK.
ERIC	I grew up with every opportunity; the best school, the best university and the best rucksack and tog factor when I travelled indifferent to each country. Then in Prague, before Thatcher surfed in on a wave of Coca Cola capitalism, I was walking along the King Charles the Fourth bridge when I was drawn towards a metallic tink hypnotising quite a large crowd. I jostled to the front to get a better view, then buckled to the

human within me. A man was hammering a six-inch nail up his nostril for money.

I'd never seen anything quite like it before. I'd shunned the addicts in Kings Cross and passed by the beggars on O'Connell Bridge but never before had I seen a man nail his brain for money. More than disgust, I felt a shame... ashamed... guilty. When I got back to Britain I felt that I had to escape from everything that I was, everything that had been thrust upon me. So I went to Oxfam, bought some suitable clothes and submerged myself in the exorcising gutter, I turned to poetry as a literary emetic, and attempted to cleanse the guilt within.

I wanted to free myself of every form of man's dominion over man, and then I met you and I realised that to truly achieve this, I must love a woman. I must love you, Dora. Will you marry me?

WOMAN (*disbelief*) What?

ERIC Is that a yes or a no?

WOMAN Watch my unsilenced lips. No.

ERIC What's wrong with me?

WOMAN Nothing's wrong with you.

ERIC Am I good-looking?

WOMAN You're all right.

ERIC Am I intelligent?

WOMAN You think.

ERIC   Do I smell?

WOMAN   Yes, but that's not the problem.

ERIC   I would be committed to you.

WOMAN   You should be committed.

ERIC   I'll divorce myself from the muse, give up poetry, buy a time share, anything to make you love me!

WOMAN   Just pin back your lug 'oles Eric and listen to me. En Oh means No. Full stop. End of discussion, do you understand?

Pause.

ERIC   So you won't marry me then?

Woman looks in disbelief.

ERIC   Yes?

WOMAN   No.

ERIC   No?

WOMAN   No.

ERIC   No!

WOMAN   No! We're just friends, Eric.

ERIC   Friends! I've just opened my heart to you.

WOMAN You've opened nothing but a can of worms in your own mind.

ERIC I've unzipped my emotions like an anorak. I've offered you my love.

WOMAN Please take it back.

ERIC I don't want it back.

WOMAN Well, I'm sorry but I don't want it.

ERIC Don't give me sympathy, just marry me.

WOMAN No.

ERIC Please reconsider.

WOMAN It's not worth the initial consideration.

ERIC You're making a fool out of me.

WOMAN You're making a fool out of yourself.

ERIC You're laughing at me.

WOMAN I'm not.

ERIC I'm sad and you're laughing at me.

WOMAN Well, I've had enough of making other people happy! From now on I'm only concerned with the future of my baby and me. That's my final word on the subject, I'm sorry, Eric.

ERIC   You will be.

WOMAN   My final word.

ERIC   You'll regret this.

WOMAN   Will I.

ERIC   Yes.

WOMAN   I don't think so.

ERIC   You will.

WOMAN   For God's sake. Emrys, I've made up my mind. Please can we get on with the baptism.

EMRYS   My pleasure.

WOMAN   Is it a quick affair?

EMRYS   Very quick.

WOMAN   And simple?

EMRYS   Very simple, though with one main difference.

WOMAN   What is that?

EMRYS   The entire ceremony. Things develop organically, and are defined and redefined if and when necessary. I call this 'The Hamburger theology'.

WOMAN   I'm all for change.

EMRYS   Good. For too long we have yoked ourselves to a sacred bullock. I feel it is time to kill the fatted calf and create traditions anew.

WOMAN   Is it legal?

EMRYS   The baptism will be legally binding in the eyes of the true God. The god of poetry.

WOMAN   What good is that to me?

EMRYS   Poetry is more powerful than any arm of state, more powerful than any transient love or other decrepit human emotion. Poetry is the word that changes the world. And if your child is baptised in the name of the muse, who knows what she might achieve?

WOMAN   My child needs every advantage.

EMRYS   Exactly, it's a dog-eat-dog world out there.

WOMAN   Admittedly, admittedly... But first, tell me more about the ceremony.

EMRYS   It comes in two parts; first the fire, then the passage.

WOMAN   I'm not so keen on the the fire bit, is it really necessary?

EMRYS   It's imperative. The immortal flame is the spark of inspiration, cleansing and renewing.

WOMAN   Is it?

EMRYS   First the child is passed over a flame...

WOMAN   For God's sake!

EMRYS   A very small flame; for irony I use England's Glory.

WOMAN   And the passage?

EMRYS   Having been purified by the flame, your child will pass through death only to be renewed and reborn in the eternity of nature.

WOMAN   I would prefer the crying and the three drops of water.

EMRYS   Beggars can't be choosers.

WOMAN   As long as you don't harm my baby.

EMRYS   Believe me, Promise means more than the world to me. Let us prepare for the ceremony. Fergus!

Fergus rings his bell. Emrys takes Eric aside.

EMRYS   Eric.

ERIC   What?

EMRYS   Will you help me?

ERIC   Yes. No one has the right to crumple my emotions and toss them like bad verse to the bin.

EMRYS   Exactly.

ERIC   I was sacrificed on the altar of my naked sincerity.

EMRYS   Painful.

ERIC Like Samson, John and Holofernes I lost my head to love. Never again will a woman do that to me.

EMRYS I should hope not.

ERIC So, I have re-consecrated my life to the muse, retaken my vows of poetry. I throw my all in with you. I will help you possess poetic perfection providing you allow me to glean from its beauty by proxy...

EMRYS Let me welcome you aboard the SS Poeticus. We will kiss perfection on both cheeks in a pincer movement upon the carcass. So let us go then you and I, let us possess the essence of creation; poetic perfection. We shall get drunk on ultimate beauty like Modigliani or Da Vinci.

WOMAN Please, Emrys. Time is getting on.

EMRYS Don't worry.

WOMAN The day is short.

EMRYS I know.

WOMAN It'll soon be night.

EMRYS I anticipate a new dawn.

WOMAN At any second my bottle-washing husband could pop round a corner and ali bomper everything.

EMRYS Over my dead body.

WOMAN He's a big man.

EMRYS   Big's irrelevant to what I'll be.

WOMAN   I'm trusting you, Emrys.

EMRYS   Believe me, I know exactly what I'm doing.

WOMAN   I hope so.

EMRYS   Hope doesn't enter into the equation. This is fate; word after word as it's meant to be.

WOMAN   Was I meant to meet you?

EMRYS   Of course you were.

WOMAN   God! If I'm not duped by men I'm duped by destiny.

EMRYS   It's the order of things, Dora.

WOMAN   Well the order stinks.

EMRYS   Perhaps it does, but who are we to question the perfumes of fate? Let the ceremony begin, it's getting late. Eric!

WOMAN   Wait. I don't want him to be a part of this!

EMRYS   He's a poet, he must play his part.

WOMAN   Let him play his part somewhere else.

EMRYS   He is vital to the whole modus operandi.

WOMAN   He is as vital as rickets.

EMRYS   I cannot baptise Promise alone, without Eric there will be no ceremony.

WOMAN   Can't Fergus help?

EMRYS   He's not a poet.

WOMAN   Oh... all right then, let's get on with it.

EMRYS   Excellent.

ERIC   Thank you.

WOMAN   Of all things, please don't thank me.

Emrys strikes a match.

WOMAN   Oh my baby. For God's sake why am I playing along with this?

EMRYS   Fight fire with fire Dora, you know it makes sense. By naming Promise you will secure her. This isn't a child's game, Dora.

WOMAN   It's a man's game.

EMRYS   It's a man's world. Baptise your baby and no bottle washing, Sodapopping man will ever be able to part you.

She begins to think.

WOMAN   This is ridiculous.

EMRYS   Deep down you know it makes sense.

WOMAN   I don't know what the hell makes sense any more.

EMRYS   Come on, Dora. Give Promise to me... Let's get on with the ceremony.

WOMAN   Hang about.

EMRYS   Time's getting on.

WOMAN   Wait.

EMRYS   Time waits for no man.

WOMAN   I am not a man, it can wait for me!

EMRYS   Come on, Dora.

WOMAN   I can't think straight.

EMRYS   Don't think, Dora. Just give me Promise. Hand her over. Let me name her. Please, Dora. Come on.

WOMAN   I'm not so sure.

EMRYS   I've wasted enough time.

WOMAN   You've wasted time!

EMRYS   Give me Promise!

WOMAN   No! I've had enough of this stupidity. Whether I name Promise or not she will always belong to me.

EMRYS   Is that your final decision?

WOMAN   Yes.

EMRYS   Then we shall seize the baby. Eric! Fergus!

Fergus grabs the woman and restrains her. Video on. Emrys and Eric perform a ceremony with a knife. Eric holds the box. Emrys stabs a knife into it.

WOMAN   No!

Blackout. The video comes on. Deafening music integrates into the 'no'. The two poets are deafened to death. The woman frees herself and reclaims her violated baby. She rocks the baby, whilst weeping. Fergus is distraught. He notices the video

HEAD   It's not bad here since all the bees of Annwn buzzed off into the world to descend upon the twiglets of another party.

The Head reveals his true identity to Fergus. It is Fergus himself. The woman sees this..

HEAD   Good riddance to the flaccid flies that deconstruct the aesthetics of effluent and the relevance of nothing. But, the 'isms' are on the wing, so I guess I'd better get going.

WOMAN   You stupid man! (*The Woman slaps Fergus' face.*)
        The purest poetry is never voiced. That which is voiced is merely second best.

Fergus realises too late that he is in fact hope.

FERGUS Wait!

HEAD   I can't wait I'm sorry; Despair's doldrum blues demand my harmony! But God, I've harmonised to some depressing songs in my time; songs to make a deaf post weep, songs as sad as crab shells boiling. But nothing compares with silence, nothing compares with nothing, nothing is as beautiful as no-sound; the sound of one hand clapping - I am the violent blind and the uncoy carp stroking a Glissando on an Empty Harp...

The Head in the video is released into the world.

Hawlfraint/Copyright Ian Rowlands January 1994

GLISSANDO ON AN EMPTY HARP

BEING IN A BELL

Declan Gorman
February 1999

A peasant character in William Carleton's nineteenth-century satire *Denis O' Shaghnessy Going to Maynooth* declared to the verbose young clerical student, Denis, that he "must have a head like a bell to hold in all them ideas". Sometimes, sitting in the tiny black box theatre at the City Arts Centre in Dublin, watching and listening to Ian Rowlands' plays, I used to feel as though I was inside a bell, where - to quote from Ian himself - "things dart about like words flailing for sentences in the napalm of 'isms'."

To be in a Theatr y Byd audience was to duck and weave and reach and catch as a scattergunload of verbal gags, metaphysical conceits, coarse jokes, politicial asides and brilliant wit ricoheted around you. Afterwards in the pub - in the hospitality of the greatest philosopher of them all, the late and legendary Ned Scanlan, publican - Ian would ask me, "What did you think?" and I'd say, "I didn't. You didn't give me time!" It is a particular pleasure to be able to revisit and reflect on his work now, in book form.

Some plays - many Irish plays actually - read exceptionally well and gain little added value in the staging. A lot of mainland European theatre work lives mainly in the performance and the text is useful primarily as a pragmatic record. Ian Rowlands' work, however, sings on the stage and resonates in these pages. You catch the notes you missed, so to speak.

For the reader for whom this book is the first introduction to Rowlands' work, I entreat you to try sometime, somewhere to catch him on tour. About as easy as lassooing a leprechaun, I should think, given the unorthodox touring route which Theatr y Byd has taken in the past. Worth pursuing, nonetheless, because Rowlands' giddy, high-speed delivery as an actor in his own plays, and the gleeful batting back of his collaborators - especially the affable Dafyd Wyn Roberts - was a critical layer in the texture of his work. As of course was the collaborative inputs of composers and visual artists who contributed to the staging.

Glissando on an Empty Harp was the third in a trio of plays which Theatr y Byd brought to the City Arts Centre, during my tenure there. I thought it was a return to humourous form on the author's part. The earlier *Solomon's Glory* had been a trifle too esoteric for my taste, after the lunacy of *The Sin Eaters* which had an almost Laurel and Hardy-like populist flavour knitting the deeper meditations together.

Glissando on an Empty Harp, according to an author's note I read somewhere, "deals with the male appropriation of art and nature". Hmmmm. This is thin ice under a company which I always felt had a particular kind of manly ethos at its core. It is better approached as an introspective rather than objective treatment of its declared theme. As such, it is hilarious and - disconcertingly - quite moving in parts.

Eric and Emrys, the main cypher-characters, are two perfectly amoral, self-serving "tramp bards" - poets acutely aware of but greedily indifferent to the absurdism and cruelty of the society they see above their hobo's embankment. They are abhorrent in their greed and forgiveable by their penury - and anyway, they get their good old-fashioned come-uppances towards the end. Dora is the hard-bitten, earthy-but-vulnerable woman visitor. Her baby - born in a grotesque stage dumbshow - is a cardboard box of dreams. This is mad stuff, thrown into relief by the sad, silent bell-ringer, Fergus, and the philosophising Head, the tired and mutilated soul in the dream box.

Metaphysics meets the Marx Bothers. This is a Celtic wordplay for which you could - if you wanted - deduce a linguistic and philosophical lineage that might include Shakespeare's clowns, Joyce's cornerboys, Beckett's outcasts, even Webster's malcontents and a dozen more, many named transparently in Rowlands' own texts. But his writing owes as much to his own passionate, living enquiry as it does to dusty texts. Whether debating the artist-audience dynamics of touring unusual (some would say difficult) plays to vastly diverse communities, or listening in to local anecdotes in West Mayo or Glamorgan, or pondering Eternity, or wondering why they put that particular silly bugger in the front row (of the Wales rugby team, not the theatre audience!), the think-atoms always appear to be careering around in his artist's bell of a head. Catch a few of his word games here in this publication and savour them while they are fresh. I suspect that in a generation's time, they will be quoting him in the Toastmaster's Companion - "On Love, let's see ... Wilde, Coward, ah, Rowlands ... 'Will you marry me?' he said, 'butter freezing in his mouth'!

Declan Gorman is Artistic Director of Upstate Theatre Project, based in Drogheda. He was formely theatre director at Dublin's City Arts Centre. He has written, directed, acted and produced and has been centrally involved in the development of the independent theatre movement in Ireland since the mid 1980's.

A FULL PRODUCTION HISTORY

IN SEARCH OF TREGARON MAN - One week's touring around Wales. Premiered Old New Inn, Llanfyllin 1/5/89

JEAN AND MI9 - One week's touring around Wales. Premiered 1/91

THE GREAT ADVENTURES OF RHYS AND HYWEL PARTS 1-4
The above, along with SOMETHING COMES OF NOTHING and CONSUMATUM EST in rep at the 4 Bars Inn, Cardiff. Theatr y Byd's first performances in Ireland 17/11/91

THE SIN EATERS - Co-production with Wales Actors' Co. 3 country tour. Premiered at Theatr Elli, Llanelli 9/4/92

SOLOMON'S GLORY - First major tour of the company in its own right. Premiered at the City Arts Centre, Dublin 26/1/93

HANFODION HAGAKURE - One week tour of Wales. Premiered Codi'r Hwyl, Bangor (Hwyl a Fflag) 5/3/93

GOGONIANT SOLOMON -Welsh adaptation of SOLOMON'S GLORY. Performed at The National Eisteddfod, Neath 1993

GLISSANDO ON AN EMPTY HARP - 4 country tour Spring 1994. Premiered Taliesin Arts Centre, Swansea 3/3/94

QUARTET - Extensive tour of Wales. 4 monologues in rep. Premiered Y Tabernacl, Machynlleth 26/8/94

THE SIN EATERS - Mounted specifically for the Carrefour d'Europe, Nantes 4/95

LOVE IN PLASTIC - Site specific production in conjunction with the Glynn Vivian Gallery, Swansea. Premiered 25/5/95

THINKING IN WELSH - Short re tour to Ireland and France of a re-working of one of the QUARTET productions. 19/3/96

LOVE IN PLASTIC - Tour of Wales and Ireland 5/96

MARRIAGE OF CONVENIENCE - Short two week tour of Wales. Premiered Coleg Meirion Dwyfor, Dolgellau 19/11/96

LLUDW'R GARREG - First ever adaptation of a Quebecois play into Welsh. Adapted by Gareth Miles from *Cendres de Cailloux* by Daniel Danis. Premiered Sherman Theatre, Cardiff 6/2/97

MARRIAGE OF CONVENIENCE - Re-tour opening at the Edinburgh Festival 8/8/97. Toured Wales, Scotland and Ireland.

MARRIAGE OF CONVENIENCE - A third six week tour. Wales, England and Ireland. February / March 1998

BLUE HERON IN THE WOMB - Collaboration with The Tron Theatre, Glasgow. Premiered 21/5/98

BLUE HERON IN THE WOMB -Welsh tour, April '99.

Future work includes a quartet of Rowlands' one act plays *The Territory of the Heart* to be performed as a residency at the Blackwood Miners' Institute. (June 1999), a new play by Rowlands, *New South Wales* to premiere at the Edinburgh Festival 1999 prior to an extensive tour and The National Eisteddfod commissioned play in Llanelli 2000. (Theatr y Byd is the first ever project based company to be granted this honour. The piece will be Rowlands' first full-length play in the Welsh language.)

Trilogy of Appropriation

Retrospective

Ian Rowlands has had over fifteen stage plays produced in the last ten years - some kind of record, I suspect, even if several are short pieces and most for his own Theatr y Byd company. I still remember my first encounter with his work, *Solomon's Glory*, in 1993; his *Ponty Trilogy* for the Sherman lunchtime theatre seasons (notably *The Ogpu Men*) stood out from the overall blandness of the radio and television product; *Marriage of Convenience*, a 1996 one-hander, remains one of the most lyrical, angry, succinct and eloquent explorations of the relationship between Wales and its neighbouring colonial power within an autobiographical narrative. None are in this volume; instead here we have three plays that I did not realise were a trilogy until *Blue Heron in the Womb* was described as the final part. *Glissando on an Empty Harp* was first produced in 1994; *Love in Plastic* dates from 1995; *Blue Heron in the Womb* is the latest version of a play that opened in 1998 and in this form toured in 1999.

When we see Rowlands's plays we have to admire the vigorous intellect, the fascination with words, the sharp wit, the very funny one-liners, the desire to form a different kind of theatre, the uncompromising dedication. His work has moved from what could seem self-indulgent wordplay to a genuine interrogation of the value of words within power relationships and from relatively simplistic politics to a more complex debate about patriarchy and patriotism.

Reading the work is, of course, a very different experience to seeing the productions. As you reach this retrospective, you have been involved in a pursuit that is not the same as that of a theatre audience. You have invested in the printed word, preserved between covers, in typographical configurations that will never change even if their meaning might. You can take down the book from the shelf whenever you want. You can pause in the middle of a page rather than at the end of an act. You can reread a speech. You can flip back to check if you missed something. You can even, if you wish, and it is the privilege of the reader denied to the theatre audience, start by turning to the last page of each play to see how it ends. We are discussing here script, not performance text, literature as much as drama.

And so to the simple immediate fact: the work is not easy to read. It is difficult, at times impenetrable, often, perhaps, the personal dressed up as the political. You have just finished reading three plays jointly entitled *Trilogy of Appropriation:* just what does this title mean ? Simply England's appropriation of Wales ? Within the plays the notion of appropriation seems to have several meanings. What does *Glissando on an Empty Harp* mean ? Meaningless superficial virtuosity on an instrument that can never produce a sound ? *Love in Plastic* ? Bubble-wrapped anaesthetised emotion ? *Blue Heron in the Womb* ? Meaningless, unless you know your Dylan Thomas.

And the wordplay goes beyond the titles. The plays are challenging to read both for their complexity and their ambiguity. While in many ways the work is far more accessible on the page than on the stage, where we do not have the luxury of pausing or re-reading, to an extent the import - is this meant seriously or as a joke, is this comedy or tragedy, is the character a fool or a thinker ? - is communicated only in a performance directed by the playwright (which is what can happen when you are not only the writer but the director and it's your theatre company). We, as readers, can never be sure we read the scripts with the appropriate tone of voice. We read them, in fact, as literature to which we bring our own interpretation.

And who are you, dear reader, and where do you come from? All three plays are full of Welsh references, linguistic, cultural and geographic, to an extent making them at times incomprehensible to anyone who does not know the country. There are allusions to art movements, artists and the commercial art world that you need to know. The substance deals with issues to do with political theories it is useful to know if not share.

Then there is the suspicion that Rowlands is, I think trying to create almost single-handedly in Wales a dramatic form that is obsessed with language. So the work demands to be read as well as seen; it is deliberately ambiguous in its seriousness; words are used as much as texture as expression of ideas or narrative. All this only comes across when all three plays are read consecutively. And beware: as a caveat I should point out that this playfulness with words (like other aspects of his work, very postmodern !) can make it seem self-regarding; we need to accord the writer some respect and trust, for there is very serious intent here.

* * * *

In *Glissando on an Empty Harp* there are, with inevitable echoes of *Waiting for Godot*, two poet-tramps, Eric and Emyr, a mute Fergus, a woman who gives birth to a box and a head that appears only on video. I wonder if, more than *Love in Plastic*, this play works only properly when it is read and if its allusions, its jokes, its ideas get lost in performance.

How does an audience absorb, for instance, a speech like this:

"The atmosphere is confused and vicious like a swarm of hornets mating on a Pollock canvas or Christmas at Holyhead when the ferry docks to spew out the coagulated inebriates of a cross Celtic fraternity, who utilise every available wall as a pissoir al fresco. The hate is gangrenous and as thick as a Rotweiller's skull, so thick you couldn't cut it with a scythe. And the smell...a Pudding Lane melange of acrid puss of the rotting sculptures of Paris Dadaismus; as stinking and putrid as a chicken plucker's fingernails teasing life as his hairy candle spurts and flails. This is Pandora's box; the venomed apple on the tree of life, inhabited by a myriad infections and afflictions more revolting than the licking tongues of spaniels, slobbering under the milk starched crinolines of starched etiquette..."

Now some of this may be, superficially at least, quite powerful, some nonsense, some striking, some merely alliterative and much of it suggesting self-indulgence and posturing - Pollock and Dada, German, French and Italian words, Greek and Biblical myth. And in the middle of this verbiage is the key to the central thrust of the play, because the woman who gives birth to the box is called, inevitably, Dora. Again, I am not sure how the image is continued, since here the box represents to the Woman hope, to the bard-tramp the perfect poem.Pandora's box is of course full of evils. But then there is only one thing left at the bottom of the box once the evils have escaped: hope. It is a core of optimism that reappears in *Blue Heron in the Womb*.

But how much would we get from hearing this speech, just one collection of words among many ?

Love in Plastic has four characters: a seedy restaurateur and his three clients, a glamorous but mature actress who appears in detergent commercials, her slick agent and a young admirer who has asked her out to dinner. There is no real plot and the whole thing is conducted at breakneck speed with metaphors tumbling over themselves.

But did you catch the stage direction near the beginning "Harold enters dressed in a space suit" ? If you missed it, you are lost, but on stage the fact that there is a character sitting at a table wearing a space suit complete with bubble dominates visually and aurally. Reading the script does not capture the same surreal situation.

The printed text again is interesting in various ways. First, it allows us to savour the rich language, exaggeratedly high-flown and wilfully meaningless but also very funny; the element of self-parody (or parody of an Anglo-Welsh lyricism[1] which Rowlands seems to espouse as well as mock) creates a teasing ambiguity. The play to an extent is about the debasement of Welshness and language (the restaurant is called with knowing false-etymological ignorance Welsh Rarebits) and this is easier to appreciate from the script than from a performance.

There is also a self-consciousness about the dual existence of printed and performance text, a playfulness again that can only be engaged in by someone who knows that his script will be read as well as performed.

There are, for example, in a well-established playwright tradition, gags in the stage directions for the reader only - the opening lines, for example: "The lights come up on an empty restaurant. The owner has a magnifying glass. He is looking for economic recovery." And, later, when the vain actress appears, "Enter Woman pursued by ego". Very amusing; but literary, not theatrical.

Interestingly, we also find that the restaurateur's words are written phonetically - which actually makes it harder to follow on the page than on the stage. (For example, I had to read twice this exchange between the character called Man and the restaurateur: "Am I confusing you?". "Puritlikeis. I've only got one 'ead, but ywv given me enough soddin' 'eadache for two." "I'm sorry..." "Oreit, lessava shifty, kid...".) And I do not really understand why a funny line about taking the A470 to a woman's heart, a precise reference that is meaningful and amusing only for those who know the road communications history of South Wales, is spelt out in the script "The A four seven O..."

Even in *Blue Heron in the Womb*, despite its near-naturalism, there are indications that it is written to be read as much as performed. And to be read by non Welsh-speakers - at the climax to the play, as a child is born, the dialogue switches to Welsh...but with, in the published script, English translation denied to the audience. None of the characters, we discover reading the script, are designated names but listed as Man, Sister, Woman, Mother and Father. The opening stage instruction is "A man hovers six feet above Wales". At one point two speeches are given at the same time, a device that works differently in performance and in print. Readers do not have to be concerned about the theatrical problems of staging a suicide by jumping off a mountain or by drowning in the sea.

The audience does have certain advantages, however. On stage there is an emotional charge you can't get from the page. There are pregnant silences (pregnancy is an important element, made the more evident to the audience by seeing Lizzie's big belly). And the programme explains what the author means by the title of the play: "The Heron was

Dylan Thomas's symbol for death," writes the author to the audience. "Blue herons are not native to Britain, but the title has been retained as it is a direct translation from the Welsh. Death is not an end, it's an opportunity." And the perplexing title of the trilogy ? "It deals with the male appropriation of nature and art through words and violence. It is also a metaphor for the state of our 'nation'...nation !" So that's what Rowlands *intends*.

Ian Rowlands, I guess, is knowingly engaged in both literature and theatre. He writes as a writer, but he also creates as a playwright, knowing that also as director he can control how the script will have a life off the page.

As a writer, he is a wordsmith. In *Love in Plastic* a leitmotif is Welsh placenames. An early exchange: "This place is like a crypt". "It's pretty dead isn't it". "Dead darling ? It's like Port Talbot". Then, "The truth is rarely sexy, I've never put much store in it; would you if you were brought up in Blaenllechau ?". Or "Full-time lying is like a house in Trehafod...at some point it's bound to go." And the riposte to "You could get married": "I'd rather live in Llanelli". And since it's set in a restaurant, there are the running gags that mock foodies and raise the question of Welsh authenticity: the place is called Welsh Rarebits rather than the proper Welsh Rabbits and Glamorgan sausage and Laverbread curry are on the menu.

But Rowlands is a wordsmith who is also immersed in the world of art (he collects paintings) and in *Glissando* a leitmotif is the world of art: art shows, galleries, first nights, Pollock, Dada, Dali, Duchamp, Picabia, Seurat, Modigliani, da Vinci all are used as references. Sometimes you could feel it is a victim of *The Waste Land* Syndrome - it needs exhaustive footnotes to explain the imagery. But I suspect in this case they are throwaway references, jokes. Like much of his imagery, there is no real substance: the work is in the spirit of Dada. And it would be helpful for the reader/audience to know about not just art but Euclid, Pythagoras and Einstein, Nero, Lazarus, Dean Freedman, Chicago (the group not the city), Flanagan and Allen, Atlantis, Japanese Katzu, satori, St Thomas, Wagner, Tibetan prayer wheels, Camus, Kierkegaard, Fonteyn, Chinganchook, Bosnia, Pound's Cantos, Aneurin, Vesuvius, metatarsals, Prague streets, Samson, John and Holfernes, the bees of Annwn - just some of the references littering the text.

Both plays are fascinating experiments in form, of using the Welsh tradition of spoken poetic imagery in a creative and jokey sense. Reading (rather than watching and listening to) *Glissando on an Empty Harp* and *Love in Plastic,* we realise that the extravagant imagery and verbal gymnastics is simultaneously stream-of-consciousness, expressionism and pastiche.

It is what the critic Roland Barthes calls "writerly" text[2]. We have to work, whether as readers or audience, to discover meanings. Rowlands has been accused of intellect-on-the-sleeve references and a kind of sophistry that allows him to write extravagant image-laded prose with the excuse that he is ridiculing language - having the facility, he both cares about it but is suspicious of it. I assume that much of it is meant to be a joke - but one told seriously and one that expresses truths. Yes, it is a kind of literary Dada, but Dada meets Foucault and feminism. (While I appreciate the postmodernist elements of *Glissando* and *Love in Plastic*, I think I am not alone in finding *Blue Heron in the Womb* a more mature and interesting play precisely because it abandons the meaningless language.) Like all "writerly" texts, Rowlands's work, as we have seen, is playful, self-conscious, concerned with the style and form, knowingly "literary". The value of Barthes's "writerly" texts (Joyce's work being an obvious example) is that they invite the reader to join in the business of producing meaning rather than treating them as a consumer. I am not sure whether Rowlands, ironically, does not actually exclude the reader from this creative process.

* * * *

So to get to the nitty-gritty. Just what is this *Trilogy of Appropriation* about ? And can we negotiate more or fewer meanings from the written text than from a performance ?

I reiterate that I deal here not with theatre but with dramatic literature, although (as you have seen) I have drawn upon the experience of seeing productions. The semiotics of performance allow audiences to find their own meanings in productions; we have here the cold printed word but it is possible to find more significance in this than in a single performance. We can, for example, look at these three plays as an entity - a trilogy, indeed, as described by the playwright. We can look for connections between the three plays.

Indeed, as a man who buys art Rowlands should be sympathetic to the view that to understand a playwright properly we should treat him as we do artists, writers and composers and look at his *oeuvre* - his total output and each play within the context of that output. We would see, maybe, not only development but recurring elements, from the repeated use of "Alex" as a name (and authorial alter-ego ?) to the use of the female as a challenge to the accepted norm and the metaphor of marriages and births to discuss political relationships. And while we can take the critical position that "there is nothing outside the text", we cannot but detect much of the personal in his *oeuvre*: the monologue *Marriage of Convenience,* for example, reads like a slice of detailed autobiography, as does at a fictional remove much of *Blue Heron in the Womb* (where, significantly, the text we have in this volume differs from that of the original production, which could have been seen as almost confessional). We may see some irony in the very fact that Rowlands is himself that ideologically-suspect of men, a collector (of artworks), an appropriator of other people's visions. But a detailed discussion of Rowlands's *oeuvre* is far more than we have space for here: let us confine ourselves to the *Trilogy* and not be tempted into looking for the life of the artist.

Glissando is clever and plays with the clichés of a Welsh-english (The english of South Wales) language and the Dadaist device of using freeflow nonsense, and is splattered with literary, geographic, artistic, musical, philosophic and historic references requiring a weighty glossary.

It seems to be saying that woman's act of creation - giving birth - is far greater than anything mere male poets can achieve. Emyr's gift is to elevate the simple act of public peeing: "I was writing the night's saga upon some wall or other with the yellow ink of my mounting pen - etching a dada masterpiece which melted like Trade Unions in winter..." But then, it is also about hope.

That use of two tramps will not only remind us of *Waiting for Godot;* the introduction of a female outsider who challenges male assumptions ensures that Gwenlyn Parry's best work is also evoked. Parry's *Saer Doliau*, which caused such a furore at the 1966 Aberfan Eisteddfod, represented a turning point in Welsh theatre; *Y Ffin*, nearly ten years later, again had two tramps and a disruptive woman in a Godot-like landscape, exploring the idea of the border; *Y Twr* (1979) tackled the loss of values in modern Wales. So is *Glissando* Rowlands's homage to the first real modern playwright of Wales ? Or is it an ironic critique, the very title suggesting that Parry's radical departure was more formalist than political ?

Love in Plastic is often very funny but its real concerns (made the clearer here by being able to read the other plays) of male oppression through language and an uncertain sense of cultural identity can seem obscured.

Blue Heron in the Womb is something different altogether. Twin sisters have had a simultaneous relationship with the same man; the one has a baby which is subsequently killed in a car crash at the age of six months; she is now pregnant again. The play is set on the day, one year after his birth, the ashes of the dead child are taken by the sisters and their parents to be scattered from an urn. The sisters, in between scenes, address many of their words to the absent male as they go into flashback.

This is more complex than the other two plays and, on first reading, more difficult partly because it is a tangled web of a story, partly because the twin sisters are simply called Woman and Sister in the script, partly because the form is deceptively close to naturalism.

It is far more overtly erotic: Sister's "Isn't it weird how the world periscopes when your crotch moistens and your pupils dilate" or "Harmonising with your cock and the clock, I screamed bitch songs at the top of my voice as revenge burst my clitoris" presumably express empowerment of sexuality by the female younger generation. But it is also provocative. How, many might ask, can a male writer put such sexually explicit language into the mouths of his female characters ? While criticising male appropriation of women, Rowlands exercises his power as author to appropriate his female characters.

The anti-male argument is more developed than *Love in Plastic* and *Glissando* and also more overt, with Mother the victim of an earlier generation's patriarchy: "I've learnt negativity from you, as most women do," are her first words. "Your values became 'our' values." Later she says:

"I blame myself for my silence when I should have spoken...my womb shrivelled with humiliation; my vagina closed and my breasts flattened. You had desexed me with a few unwitting words not meant to offend ...it was just another statement that rolled off your tongue, unchallenged by a silent woman.."

Her husband represents not merely oppressive patriarchy but old-fashioned romantic nationalism and religious bigotry:

"They say babies gurgle in dialect, rehearsing the language they will eventually speak. If this is true, then Welsh babies are doubly blessed, for their gurglings are not only the formative sounds of the divine tongue, but their linguistic passports to life everlasting...";
he represents, perhaps, in his old-fashioned religiosity, his rigidity and simplistic nationalism, much that is wrong with "old" Wales.

Blue Heron is the nearest Rowlands gets to naturalism. There is a sort of narrative, or rather two narratives: one, the present as the family scatters the ashes of the dead child, the other the past as the sisters tell the connected histories of their relationship with their shared lover. There are very dramatic moments. There is emotion. The dialogue is realistic. The characters are believable.

Superficially it is a domestic tragedy. But it is also a metaphor for Wales - as the family so often is, the father representing the oppression by patriarchy, extreme nationalism and the church, the twins representing a divided nation, with the image of the storms that flattened much of the country coinciding with the birth of the baby, the promise of a new birth to come - with its changing attitudes. It is also, of course, about sexual politics, about the abuse of women by men in two generations told from three women's points of view (the men hardly get a look in).

* * * *

The three plays have been successful as individual works, but they take on more when seen as a trilogy. We cannot but be intrigued and beguiled by the interweaving of sexual politics, culture, nationalism, black comedy and slapstick, even if not everybody is altogether convinced by the implied arguments that language can be both an expression of male power but also meaningless, with an implied ironic contradiction in that Rowlands seems to be using his (male) fluency and erudition to argue that men oppress women with words.

But undeniably the *Trilogy of Appropriation* is evidence of the development of an artist who, I believe, has something interesting and exciting to offer Welsh culture. Perhaps *Blue Heron* works best as a play, whether conceived to be read or seen, as it brings to a head the political debates, where a Wales obsessed with language, with religion, with xenophobic nationalism, with patriarchy, is used through the metaphor of drama.

What we have here is a trio of texts that explore Welshness - not in any negative jokey way nor in any sociological study but from the political perspective of a people dominated by a colonising neighbour. This is manifest not in narrative or setting but through a variety of strategies.

Rowlands's concern is the state of the nation. But as with other writers describing the relation between colonising power and oppressed nation he talks not about politics but sexual relationships. Like Doris Lessing (in an African context), Toni Morrison (in a black American context) or Margaret Atwood (in a Fourth World Canadian context), Rowlands makes men and women, the dominator and dominated, analogous to the coloniser and colonised. The links between imperial power and patriarchy are well-rehearsed (including the dominance of the male gaze, potently evoked in Wales in phrases like The Rape of the Fair Country[3]) but Rowlands goes further, as we have seen, and can make men synonymous with guilt and blame. Sometimes this is a familiar recourse to feminist ideas of patriarchy but there is also the suspicion that a more personal perception is operating, particularly in *Blue Heron*.

At the heart of Rowlands's techniques, though, as I have suggested, is the use of language. On one level, it is very complex. But it is also very Welsh: Rowlands is a Welsh speaker (evidenced in several plays, notably *Marriage of Convenience*) and he addresses an audience (and readership) assumed to be Welsh or familiar with Welsh references. In some ways he can be seen as part of a tradition that can be traced back to J O Francis, Caradoc Evans and Dylan Thomas; his work can also be seen as an example of a genre of writing that tries to mediate cultural nationalism through a specific literary and theatrical style.

Critics exploring the phenomenon detectable in recent indigenous work from the so-called Third and Fourth Worlds use the term "syncreticism"[4] to describe how the language and culture of the powerful colonising nations can be adopted and used by the dominated peoples (the idea of syncreticism is borrowed from comparative religion to denote the process whereby elements of one religion are absorbed into another and redefined). Chris Balme, the New Zealand academic and theatre historian, uses "syncretic theatre" as a framework within which to discuss Maori drama. Theatrical Syncreticism, in Balme's theory, is "a conscious strategy to fashion a new form of theatre in the light of colonial or postcolonial experience", common in Africa and the Caribbean and increasingly so in Fourth World cultures in New Zealand, Australia and Canada.[5.]

Maori theatre clearly, like Rowlands's work, abrogates the colonists' culture: that is, it rejects English theatre models and forms, as well as standard English, as the aesthetic and ideological "norm". Rowlands does this by using non-naturalist styles, by emphasising Welsh vernacular speech, by incorporating Welsh literature, myth and social references. Abrogation is a crucial step towards creating an indigenous theatre, but this refusal is not enough. To re-possess the culture a new lanuage has to be used.

Syncretic theatre is therefore about appropriation - the appropriation of the language of the dominating power. There is, of course, a living theatre practice in the Welsh language: Ian Rowlands is in fact writing the Eisteddfod commission for a new play for the year 2000. The sort of syncreticism I identify in Wales is one where the work is not in the mother tongue but in that of the colonising power. Some Welsh playwrights have appropriated the English language - or rather aspects of the language - to good effect, not unlike Shakespeare's Caliban who, having been taught Prospero's English (Elizabethan New World explorers knew that colonial power started with the imposition of their language as much as did their Victorian descendants)[6.], therefore knew how to curse him. Some, like Rowlands, invent a language that is as unEnglish, or as subversively similar to standard English, as the "english"[7.] of Fourth World writers. What the Welsh syncretic theatre writers achieve is a language that is distinctively Welsh english (sometimes ambiguously labelled Anglo-Welsh), in vocabulary, rhythm, syntax, sentence structure and sound. This may be often filled with references to Bardic poetry and Celtic folklore. It can be allied to a subversion of styles of English drama like naturalism. The resultant syncretic form is used effectively to explore questions of cultural identity, domination, dispossession and annexation.

The crucial value of syncretic theatre is its ability to "decolonise the stage". This is just what Rowlands is doing. He deploys language by abrogating and appropriating standard English. But he is essentially also theatrical; reading these play scripts, with the close attention to the text that reading allows, can in many ways be more rewarding than seeing them. If we only read the scripts, however, we miss out on some dramatic qualities that also define his work and his cultural strategies, qualities emphasised by the fact that to date he has always directed his own work. Because he also abrogates and appropriates theatrical convention by subverting the traditional naturalism of English theatre. He emphasises the Welshness of his plays by reference to place names, food, cultural history and so on, and by using Welsh. He empowers (controversially and perhaps problematically) women by allowing them to appropriate the sexually explicit language of men.[8] He uses comedy, and especially black comedy, as part of this battery of weapons.

Some say that Ian Rowlands is the best playwright Wales has. Certainly Rowlands is an original but at the same time we can see in his work many of the elements that identify an emergent new Welsh theatre. Crucially, he is using ideas and images of Welshness in both comic and serious ways to explore the immediate and the universal - and his plays undeniably deserve to be read and repay repeated reading. Perhaps it is time to turn back to the beginning of this *Trilogy of Appropriation* and begin again.

David Adams April 1999

Notes

1 Anglo-Welsh is a problemmatic phrase. I do not mean the deliberate creation of an "English" that is actually Welsh, but more the use of English with a Welsh accent.

2 Barthes discusses "writerly" (*scriptable*) and "readerly" *(lisible)* texts in *S/Z*.

3 I explore how Wales was perceived by an imperialist England as part of a patriarchal "orientalising" power discourse in *Stage Welsh* (Gomer 1996).

4 See Ashcroft, Griffiths and Tiffin, *The Empire Writes Back* (Routledge 1989) for an introduction to Postcolonial theory and practice. "Postcolonial theory and practice. "Postcolonial writing defines itself by seizing the language of the centre and re-placing it in a discourse fully adapted to the colonised place."

5 See Balme, *Between Separation and Integration* in *The Intercultural Performance Reader* (Routledge 1996). In an uncomfortably academic style, he defines syncertic theattre as 'the amalgamation of indigenous performance forms with certain conventions and practices of the Euro-American theatre tradition, to produce new theatrico-aesthetic principles". There are obvious similarities between Maori theatre and Welsh theatre. Maori theatre is relatively recent (like Wales, where professional theatre has existed only for thirty years or so); traditionally there was no Maori "dramatic enanactment" (ditto Wales). "As in many nonscribal societies" (Wales's culture is essentially oral, "the theatrical experience...was in fact catered for by a set of cultural performances which involved a high degree of theatricality" (as in Wales, where performance took the form of rituals preserved in folk customs like the Mari Lwyd) governed by a strict set of 'rituals of encounter'.

6 See Greenblatt's *Learning How to Curse* (Routledge 1990) for a fascinating exploration of the Elizabethan explorers' use of language as an essential part of the colonisation project.

7 The lower case "e" is to differentiate between language as an expression of the colonising power and as the spoken or written word.

8 A reminder that women can be seen to have been "colonised": there is a burgeoning academic practice that links postcolonialist and feminist critiques. See Gayatri Spivak *In Other Worlds* (Methuen 1987).

Trilogy of Appropriation